"Sandy—I need

"I don't want to _____ _____ said. "You'd better take me home."

Bill abruptly turned around in a parking lot he was passing and headed back toward her house. His expression was grim, almost angry. "I'd be better for you, Sandy. Your mother thinks so, too."

Anger replaced her anxiety. "How do you know what my mother thinks? I hope you and she didn't discuss this!"

"Just a little, last night before you came downstairs. She didn't say much, but I could tell how she felt." He pulled up in front of her house. "We both worry about you with Jeff. It's not just that we think this won't last…"

"Why else should you worry?"

Bill hesitated. "For one thing, he has a temper. He may physically hurt you. Remember how he was even as a kid."

Her anger notched up higher. He was sounding just like her mother, expressing unfounded, outdated fears. "It was years ago that he got in those fights. He's not like that now. I'm sorry, Bill, but I think it would be better if you and I don't see each other for a while." She got out of the car and slammed the door.

Bill started to pull away, then stopped, lowered the window, and called out to her. "Just remember, if you ever need me, I'll be here."

Praise for Patricia McAlexander

Stranger in the Storm:
"Congratulations on the Crowned Heart of Excellence review….It takes a lot of hard work and perseverance to write a story of such caliber."

~ *InD'tale Magazine*

"A wonderful romance thriller. This story is filled with twists, turns, and suspense."

~ *Still Moments Magazine*

"A page-turner…It could become a movie."

~ *Jerome Loving,*
author of Jack and Norman

Shadows of Doubt:
"Sandy Harris discovers the deceptiveness of appearances in this coming-of-age novel involving the dark underworld of college drug dealing…At once chilling and literary."

~ *Molly Hurley Moran,*
author of Finding Susan

". . .A thought-provoking story. Author gives the reader a satisfying romance with contemporary predicaments and complex characters. . ."

~ *Julie Howard,*
author of the Wild Crime
and Spirited Quest series

Shadows of Doubt

by

Patricia McAlexander

Shadows of Doubt

Cover Art by *Rae Monet, Inc.*

The Wild Rose Press, Inc.
PO Box 708
Adams Basin, NY 14410-0708
Visit us at www.thewildrosepress.com

Publishing History
First Edition, 2021
Trade Paperback ISBN 978-1-5092-3542-1
Digital ISBN 978-1-5092-3543-8

Published in the United States of America

Dedication

To my sister Dorothy, my son Edward, my husband Hubert, and my friend Jane—all early readers of this novel.

Prologue

After school, as usual, third-grader Sandy Harris walked down the corridor to the fifth-grade classroom at the end of the hall where her mother taught. A slight girl with curly blonde hair, glasses, and, many people said, a pretty face, she would help her mother clean the boards and straighten the desks. Then, they would ride together to their home in the university town of Athens, Georgia. Sometimes, a student in the class, Bill Morrison, the son of her mother's best friend and like a brother to Sandy, would help too and afterward clamber into the back seat to ride with them.

Usually, the door to her mother's classroom was wide open, with her mother moving briskly around, sometimes talking and laughing with Bill if he'd stayed to help. Today, however, something was wrong; the door was tightly closed. Sandy hesitated, then cautiously opened it a crack and peeked in. Rows of empty desks stretched to the front of the room in eerie stillness—a quiet like a pause in a storm. And there she saw her mother, standing with arms folded across her middle, glaring at a boy sitting at a desk before her. Her expression would normally frighten anyone, but the boy, though pale, just sat there, glaring back. At her interruption, both the boy and her mother turned to look at her.

Sandy recognized Jeff Hudson, another of her mother's students. Muscular and strong for his age, with unruly, dark hair, a cleft in his chin, and blazing hazel eyes, he had a bad reputation for disrupting classes, getting into fights on the playground, and spending time in the principal's office. More than once, Sandy overheard her mother tell her father, "I wonder how I'll make it through the year with *that boy*!"

As Sandy took in the sight, her mother motioned impatiently—almost angrily—for her to leave. Wondering if she should, if her mother would be all right, Sandy backed out and closed the door. But she stayed alert, standing right outside it. She could hear the sounds, though not the words, of her mother's sharp questions and the boy's brief responses. Then there came that eerie quiet again. Anxious, she stepped closer, but the door jerked open and Jeff burst out, his hard body colliding with hers. Sandy felt the breath knocked from her chest, felt herself falling backward. With quick reflexes, he reached out, caught her arms, and pulled her upright. Then, without pause or apology, he brushed on past her and disappeared down the hall.

****

"Jeffrey Hudson," said the social worker, sitting down at the table across from him, "you're how old now? Eleven?"

Jeff did not want to speak to this woman. He'd had enough of his teacher, Mrs. Harris, and school administrators questioning him after his fights, and of juvenile court officers since they'd caught him stealing from the school. They all knew how old he was. He barely nodded.

"How would you like to live permanently with

2

your mother and grandparents in Atlanta? You will still see your father after the divorce. You can visit him on weekends."

Jeff felt pressure building in his chest. "I don't want to visit him."

"Your father will want to see you."

"I don't think so."

"A boy your age needs his father."

Jeff could never forgive him for making his pretty mother cry so often, for making her drink, for making her talk about wanting to die. "I don't need mine."

The social worker tightened her lips, seeming for a moment at a loss for words. Then she said, "You may change your mind about that. But you will live with your mother and grandparents in Atlanta and go to a new school. You'd like that, wouldn't you?"

Jeff nodded again, keeping his eyes on the table. He hated that she looked at him as if he were some sort of caged wild animal.

"Your behavior has been quite a problem, especially this last year," she went on. "Now breaking into the school and stealing that money has gotten you in real trouble." She opened a folder before her. "You are lucky. The judge likes you. He seems to feel you can do better in a new environment. Your tests show that you're very intelligent. Living with your mother and your grandparents, you can have a fresh start at a private school in Atlanta, get good grades, make new friends. You and she will also have sessions with a therapist there. He'll keep an eye on how you both are doing, report to us, give you help when—and if you need it."

"Therapist? You mean a psychologist?"

"Well, yes…while we see how you're doing."

"I don't need a psychologist."

The social worker's voice turned even colder. "Your mother is willing to see him. And that's part of the deal if you go to live with her and your grandparents."

She closed the folder and stood. Jeff looked up at her, feeling his eyes burning—with anger, with repressed tears. He did not reply.

"All right, then. Your mother is waiting out in the hall. You'll go back to Atlanta with her today. To stay."

Jeff rose and followed the woman through the consulting room door. He knew one thing: he wanted never to come back to Athens.

Chapter One

Ten Years Later

Jeff Hudson idled the tractor in the turn row and reached for the bottle of water at his feet. The sun shone hot on his shoulders and the back of his neck. The strawberry field he was cultivating stretched out before him in neat rows, and above him, he saw the North Carolina blue sky he loved. But he did not feel the happiness of working on his uncle's farm that he usually did. After he'd lived here over two years, his uncle wanted to him to leave.

Not that Uncle Jake, his mother's widowed brother, felt displeased with him—quite the opposite. He said he wanted Jeff to become his partner in managing Rushing Creek Farm, the Community Supported Agriculture business which grew and sold produce to area residents and restaurants. In fact, having no children himself, his uncle said he would someday leave the entire business to Jeff. But on one condition: Jeff had to go back to school and get a degree in agriculture. And not just any school. It would have to be the University of Georgia's College of Agriculture and Environmental Sciences. Uncle Jake had attended UGA for two years, until he dropped out, his dyslexia preventing him from getting good enough grades. But he had great affection for it, nevertheless. Wearing one of his red or black Georgia shirts and a UGA baseball cap, he still often drove to Athens on football game weekends to root boisterously for the Bulldogs. Sometimes he'd get to fly there as a passenger in the twin-engine plane owned by a wealthy neighbor, an equally avid football fan.

Uncle Jake told Jeff that the University of Georgia had one of the best ag schools in the South. "You've finished three semesters at Georgia Tech," he went on. "Your grades were good. Most of your courses will transfer. So you'll only have two and a half years to go. I'll pay all your expenses. Then you can come back here as my partner in Rushing Brook. Having someone with a college degree will look good to the customers and to the banks when we apply for loans on the farm. And what you learn will be a help to me. So, that's the deal, Jeff."

He took off his wide-brimmed hat, poured some water over his thick, dark hair, and slammed the water bottle down. He did *not* want to go to the University of Georgia—not to any place in Georgia. He wanted to stay right here and work on the farm. Even now, he still had nightmarish flashbacks about his time at Tech.

Dealing had started out easily enough his freshman year—smoking weed and vaping THC offered by his upperclassman roommate, then agreeing to sell those products, as his roommate did, along with some prescription pills, for a pretty good profit. Once on a tight budget, he now had money for dates, a car, and, in his sophomore year, an apartment. He told his parents he had a part-time job, kept his grades up with no problem, stopped using drugs himself, and organized sales efficiently. The clean-cut look he'd developed in high school, along with his record as a football and track star there, kept the cops and university officials from suspecting him, while at the same time he had the physical ability to defend himself when necessary. The suppliers, pleased, kept wanting him to do more. But at the end of his freshman year, one of their dealers was murdered, his body found in the Chattahoochee River; then Jeff's roommate was arrested for dealing and expelled.

"Those two were not as smart—or as tough—as you," his suppliers said. Needing someone to fill their places, they began sending him to downtown Atlanta, even had him push cocaine a couple of times. Jeff realized he'd gotten in far deeper than he wanted to.

In the second half of his sophomore year, he was pulled over and his car searched. The officers did not find the scales, packaging, the wad of cash. He'd hidden them well with a false bottom under the spare tire. All he had left in the car was a few grams of marijuana, so they could arrest him only for possession.

The cops admitted they suspected there was more to it than that. "We're pretty sure you're trafficking— you've got drugs here somewhere," they said.

They handcuffed him and thrust him roughly into the police car. He was kept in the Fulton County Jail for several days, with bail set at the legal limit. He refused to contact either of his parents—it would have been too much for his mother, herself a recovered alcoholic; and he felt too alienated from his father. He finally called his uncle.

Jake drove down to Atlanta right away and paid his bail. But he was angry when Jeff later told him the whole story. "*Hell*, son, how could you have done this?

After you did so well with your studies. I thought after fifth grade, we'd seen the end of you getting in trouble with the law. This time you're an adult. If they'd found out what you'd been doing, you could have been sent up for years."

Jeff tried to explain how it began with just helping out his roommate, then how he became increasingly entangled—those nighttime meetings with his supplier in the abandoned factory, the expansion of his dealing responsibilities. "They weren't going to let me quit."

"Well, you are quitting—and you're getting out of here. As of today, you're withdrawing from Tech," Uncle Jake said. "Sell your car, pack up your things, close out your checking and cell phone accounts. I'll talk to the judge about taking you back to North Carolina with me."

"What about Mom? And my father?"

"I'll take care of them, too. I'll just say you've decided to take some time off from school."

Jeff was glad to obey, glad to get away from the mess he'd found himself in. And once he got to the farm, he loved it. The hard, physical labor, the companionship with Uncle Jake—not only working with him in the fields, but hiking mountain trails with him, kayaking on the rivers, hunting game in season—provided all the life he wanted.

He shook the water out of his hair, grown quite long now, replaced his hat, and put the tractor back into gear. He had argued with his uncle against leaving the farm. Uncle Jake insisted that returning to college would be good for him. He'd dismissed Jeff's concern about the old drug contacts finding him in Athens. They would've forgotten him, he said—anyway, they'd never know where he was.

Probably Uncle Jake was right. And his parents would be glad he was going back to finish his degree.

Jeff finished the last row, then drove the tractor to the barn. He turned off the engine and jumped down. His uncle was there waiting for him. "Well, son, have you been thinking any more about my offer?"

Jeff looked at his stubborn, sunburned, stringy-muscled uncle and spoke abruptly, "All right."

"All right? You'll go back to school? To the University of Georgia?"

"Do I have a choice?"

His uncle just laughed and clapped him on his sweaty shoulder. "They've been sending us information ever since your application was accepted and I said you'd go. In fact, you could start taking courses this summer."

"*This summer?*"

"The sooner you start, the sooner you graduate and come back here. There's still time to register for the summer session. You can take my old Dodge Durango to Athens. I'll hire extra help for the couple of years while you're away. I'll miss you, but I'll manage."

Shit. This was sooner than he'd expected. Jeff turned and climbed back onto the tractor to take it to the machine shed. He looked down at his uncle. "All right, then. I'll start on that damned degree this summer."

****

On a Sunday evening in early June, Mrs. Harris came out on the front porch—a tall, blue-eyed woman with glasses, no-nonsense brown hair, and the definiteness about her personality that had made her such an effective teacher and now the grade school principal. She saw her daughter sitting on the porch steps, waiting for the young man who was supposed to pick her up any minute now. "Sandy, I'm so glad you're going to see Bill tonight," she said, sitting down on the step herself.

"Yes—but it will seem strange after not seeing much of him these last four years. When he was home for vacations at Thanksgiving and Christmas, he hardly ever came by."

Mrs. Harris was quick to defend the son of her best friend. "He didn't have much time to spend here. He couldn't pass up those programs at Chapel Hill his first two summers and then that study-abroad session in Spain last year. Now that he's back for the whole summer, I'm sure it will be like old times for the two of you again." She paused. "You almost went away yourself this summer."

"I couldn't do that. Not after Dad…"

Sandy could not say it. She felt the tears begin to prickle her eyes again. She still could hardly believe he had died. She'd noticed that her father, a real estate agent, had seemed tired and stressed the past year, was not selling as many houses as he usually did. Then one day in April as he was driving home from showing a house, he'd suddenly pulled over to the curb and stopped. Cars braked and honked their horns around him. When people ran up to see what had happened, they saw his head fallen against the steering wheel. "Sudden cardiac arrest," the doctor called it.

Sandy had planned to attend a six-week photography workshop in the Smokies that summer, but she couldn't leave her mother so soon after her father's death. Mrs. Harris was outwardly a strong person, but

Sandy knew she'd depended emotionally on her husband. She'd like to have her daughter with her this summer, until school started again.

Her mother reached out now and squeezed Sandy's hand. "It's will be like old times, with you back in your room, not off in a dorm or sorority house. And now that Bill's back, this summer will be more interesting for you." She paused, regarding Sandy. "I'm sure he's even better looking now. And of course, *you've* changed since high school."

Sandy knew her mother was not talking about her becoming more independent. She was talking about her appearance. Her blonde hair, with its natural waves, had grown long, she'd had LASIK surgery, so she didn't have to wear glasses anymore, and though still slim, she had finally filled out in the right places. Sandy also recognized the matchmaking intent behind her mother's comments. Her mother—and Bill's mother too—surely had dreamed about a future for her and "Billy" when he and she were kids.

On those long, warm afternoons, while the women sat and talked, the two children played side by side in the sandbox and kiddie pool. In grade school, she and Billy went together with their parents on picnics, to Fourth of July fireworks displays, skiing in North Carolina. When they were teenagers, Bill, a year older than she, tall, lean, and studious, had sometimes taken her to dances or movies.

But there was never anything romantic between them. They were always like brother and sister. She'd dreamed of her real crushes from a distance, while Bill just didn't seem interested in dating at all—she was the only girl he ever took out. Now, since her father's death, her mother seemed particularly eager for her and Bill to reconnect—romantically. Perhaps she envisioned Bill as becoming the man of the family.

A red sports car pulled up to the curb. "Here he is!" exclaimed her mother, standing up and waving.

The car door opened, and there he stood, tall, blond, and lean still, with the same light sprinkling of freckles across his cheekbones, the same fine aristocratic nose, and striking, pale green eyes. But he was more mature and solid than he'd been four years earlier. *Mom was right*, Sandy thought. *He looks great.*

"Bill!" Her mother stood as he approached and hugged him warmly. "Welcome back to Athens. We've missed you."

"Thanks. And I've missed you." Bill returned the hug, then turned to Sandy. They hugged too.

"I was so sorry to hear about Mr. Harris," he said, stepping back. "It's hard to believe."

"Yes, it was a shock—so sudden," her mother said. "But...what a nice surprise that *you* will be spending the summer here."

"I'm doing what my parents want. I'm working at the store with my father. And playing a lot of golf with him. I'll go back to UNC for a master's degree in business this fall."

"Oh, that's wonderful," said Mrs. Harris.

"I'll be back to see you again soon. Let me know if there's anything I can do."

He hugged the woman again, then escorted Sandy to his car, opening the door for her. For a few moments after he pulled away, there was silence except for the smooth hum of the engine. Then Bill looked over at her. "Your mother seems to be doing okay."

"She's a tough lady. But it's good I decided to stay home with her this summer. She's glad I'm here."

"So what will you do this summer while you're staying with your mother?"

"I'm taking a course on Tuesdays and Thursdays— 'Early Victorian Novels by Women'—to fulfill my humanities requirement. And I have a job babysitting on Mondays, Wednesdays, and Fridays for a professor's three-year-old while his wife is abroad doing research for her dissertation. My first day is tomorrow. The job was sort of last minute. His wife's mother was supposed to keep the little boy at her house every day during the week, but she's had a knee replacement and can't do that after all."

"Who's the professor?"

"Dr. Hudson, in the anthropology department."

Bill seemed to freeze for a moment. "Dr. Hudson—Jeff Hudson's father?"

"That's right," said Sandy. "He and Jeff's mother divorced back when Jeff was in fifth grade. He's married again."

"Jeff won't be there, will he?"

"He's been gone from Athens since the divorce. I'm sure he won't be around."

Bill relaxed. "That's good. I remember him well. He started fights on the playground that fifth-grade year all the time. We never knew who Jeff would try to beat up next."

"I was two grades behind you and him," Sandy said. "We had a different recess period and never saw the fights. But I heard the stories."

"Like when he broke into school and stole some money."

13

"My mother never had a problem student like Jeff. She was so relieved when he moved away before the school year was over. She told my dad she was afraid he would end up in jail someday, wherever he was." Sandy paused, remembering how he caught her when he'd almost knocked her down outside her mother's classroom. "I wonder what *has* happened to him."

Bill pressed harder on the accelerator. "I say good riddance."

The car shot smoothly and powerfully forward. "This is a nice car," Sandy said.

"Graduation present from the parents." Bill looked at the passing streets. "This town has changed a lot in four years."

"You should have come home more often to keep up on the new additions."

"I know. Life got in the way." As they drove around the campus, Sandy pointed out the new buildings—a business school complex, a cafeteria, a student learning center. Then Bill took an unexpected turn. "Let's go to Memorial Park." He drove through town to the park entrance, and then down the dusky road to the little man-made pond, home to ducks, tadpoles, and turtles. He turned off the motor. "Shall we walk around?"

They got out of the car and went down to the edge of the pond. Most of the people had gone, and the only sounds were pond frogs and crickets in the grass. "Remember when our mothers used to bring us here to feed the ducks?"

Sandy laughed. "There was just one with a red bill. We liked him best. We called him Little Red Face."

"Let's sit on the grass. I've got a blanket."

She waited as he ran to the car, then returned and spread out the blanket. "It's getting dark," she said. "I think the park is supposed to close at sunset."

"They've never enforced that." He stretched out on the blanket. She sat down beside him. "So what's been happening to you these four years?" he asked. "Have you been dating anyone?"

"I dated someone the last half of my freshman year and the first of half of my sophomore year. We did a lot of photography work together. He graduated last December and moved to Los Angeles. He's been working on a camera crew for a movie production studio and has just been accepted into the UCLA film and media graduate program. How about you?"

He shook his head and laughed a little. "Maybe the less said about that, the better." He tilted his head back toward the sky. "Look at the stars. There's Venus, the bright one."

"The evening star."

"Your father used to tell us about the constellations when we went on those beach trips. We'd all go out by the ocean and look at the stars."

"Yes, those were good times."

They sat in silence a few minutes before Bill said, "I guess we should head back." He stood, took her hand, and helped her to her feet. Together, they folded the blanket. As they finished, coming face to face for the last fold, he said, "I think you know what my parents and your mother have always wanted for the two of us."

"Yes."

He took the blanket from her hands. "I should have kept in closer touch. We should have gotten together

15

when I came home for vacations."

"We were both busy."

Back at the car, he put the blanket into the back seat, and they got in. He punched the ignition button and drove back up the hill and to Sandy's street. After parking in front of her house, he turned to look at her. "Are you still involved with that boyfriend in LA?"

"I think it's over."

"Maybe you and I...."

Sandy waited.

"You and I need to get reacquainted. How about we go to the movie at the University Union Thursday night? I'd wait and ask you to go this weekend, but I'm going to a golf tournament in Florida with my father."

"Thursday night would be fine."

"I'll call you about the time."

She could see only the outline of his face in the darkness. "All right." She hesitated, wondering if he might give her the kind of brotherly kiss he once used to give her—or some other kind of kiss. But he did neither. "Good night," she said. Standing on the curb, she watched the glowing taillights of his car as he drove off down the street.

****

Sandy walked up the sidewalk to her house. Even if he hadn't kissed her, it seemed Bill had suggested a new kind of relationship, no longer just as brother and sister. There *was* something different about him. Had he, after four years of an almost-Ivy League school and international travel, become worldly, sexually experienced? He was certainly good looking now, in that genteel way. He was smart. Her parents had always loved him. And it was true—her mother and his parents would be so happy if they became a couple.

The light in the front hall was on. Sandy switched it off, then went quietly upstairs. As she passed her parents' room, she heard her mother getting out of bed. "Sandy?" The door opened and her mother stood there, looking sleepy without her glasses and tying the belt of her bathrobe. "Did you and Bill have a good time?"

"We did. But we'd better get to bed."

"Yes, you're going to your babysitting job tomorrow, aren't you? All right, goodnight, honey." Her mother gave Sandy a quick kiss and retreated.

In her own room, Sandy changed to a light summer nightgown and lay on her bed, thinking. She hadn't wanted to tell Bill all the details about her relationship with John Milan. But for over a year, they'd had good times together, going to plays, movies, social events, and on photo shoots. Under his tutelage, she'd learned to use her DSLR camera more effectively, applying filters and specialized lenses. She won prizes for her photos in local contests and began adding photos to the news stories she wrote for the UGA student newspaper. John, of course, had also initiated her sexually.

Bill had asked if the relationship was over. The answer wasn't clear-cut. But as the last semester had passed, she realized John now lived in a Hollywood type of world she didn't really want to be part of. When she put off going to visit him over spring break, he did not protest. And when he asked if she wanted him to fly back for her father's funeral, she said he did not need to. Yes, she thought, their paths had diverged.

Now at least her schedule for the summer was established. She'd been able to find a job even though she hadn't started looking for one there in town until the end of the semester. She liked children, had taken care of them throughout high school, and now wanted the flexibility of part-time employment. Her three-day-a-week job with Dr. Hudson would work perfectly, and Bobby seemed to be an unusually precocious, articulate child who would be fun to care for. What she didn't know was what kind of relationship would develop with Bill. And then she thought, *I really must ask Dr. Hudson what has happened to Jeff.*

Chapter Two

Jeff drove down the stretch of Lumpkin Street that ran through the University of Georgia campus. He hadn't been back to Athens for four years—not since he turned eighteen and the court order requiring him visit his father no longer applied. New multi-storied brick structures now towered up on either side of the road, but the route to the house he'd lived in with his parents as a kid and where, after the divorce, his father remained, had not changed. Driving on those streets again, he felt old tensions rising within him.

He'd lived in Athens until he was eleven. Memories of those times came back now as he drove the familiar route. His professor father being away most of the time—on weekend research trips, he claimed, or at his university office all those long evenings, supposedly writing a book to get tenure. His mother drinking innumerable glasses of wine, at first just in the evening, then during the day as well. Her telling him, in increasingly slurred words, that his father was going to abandon them, that he was in love with another woman. The shouts he heard in the nights when he did come home—his mother's hysterical voice, his father's angry one. The days after, her crying, shoulders shaking as she pulled Jeff into her arms, telling him she wanted to commit suicide. Maybe she'd go to the Watson Mill

Bridge and jump into the Oconee River. Or maybe she would get into a bathtub of hot water and slit her wrists.

He'd hated his absent father for causing his mother such pain. But all he could do to express his anger was talk back to the teachers and start fights on the playground with other boys at school—big dramatic fights everyone watched, earning him and his opponents much time in the principal's office. Then one night, he'd broken into the school and stolen some money. Upon leaving, he'd been apprehended by two policemen on patrol. That was when he'd first gotten into trouble with the law.

Now his father lived in that house of his childhood with a second wife and their child, a son about three. He'd never met either of them. Jeff knew the apartment over the garage was still there too, for Uncle Jake had contacted his father and gotten permission for him to live in it, if he wanted to, at least temporarily. The wife would be gone for most of the summer, his uncle said, doing some kind of study abroad for her PhD. His father would teach summer school, and the little boy would stay most of the time with the wife's mother. Uncle Jake clearly felt proud of setting up this possible living arrangement for him.

For weeks, Jeff delayed contacting his father about staying in the apartment. He'd had enough of those enforced visits with him years ago, of watching him with his lady friends. Who knew what he'd be doing this summer while this new wife was away? But checking repeatedly online for places to live in Athens yielded nothing. His inquiries were late, and any available apartments were expensive or inconvenient or the people advertising for roommates did not sound like people he'd want to live with. He'd learned enough about unknown roommates at Tech. His uncle pointed out again that the garage apartment would be the perfect solution, and it would be rent free.

Only the day before had he finally lowered his pride and texted his father, saying he would like to stay there for a short time. He had not received an answer. But he assumed the offer still held.

****

On Monday morning, Sandy parked her ten-year-old Toyota at the curb in front of the Hudson house. Dr. Hudson's car was parked in the driveway beside a garage that had a second story, with steps leading up to a side door. Sandy looked up at it. A garage apartment—she hadn't noticed that before. Putting the strap of her large canvas tote bag over her shoulder, she walked down the driveway to the back entrance, where she'd entered for her interview. Through the screen door, she saw Bobby at the kitchen table, a bowl of cereal in front of him. Dr. Hudson sat with him, dressed in jeans and a sport shirt—the casual wear most professors now adopted. Broad shouldered, craggy faced, with thick salt-and-pepper hair, he obviously had married a much younger woman this second time.

He rose, a worried look on his face, and opened the door for her. "Come in, Sandy." As Bobby let out a wail, he turned away from the child and spoke quietly to her. "Bobby's used to going to his grandmother's when my wife and I go away. That's why I didn't want to enroll him in a nursery school. Having you as a sitter here will be more like—"

"I don't want a babysitter. I want Grandma!" Bobby cried out, his face turning red.

Dr. Hudson turned back to his little boy. "I've told you. Grandma is getting a new knee and can't take care of you this summer after all. You liked Sandy when she came to visit us. Remember how you showed her all the toys in your room?"

Sandy found herself rising to the occasion. "Bobby, it's time for me to show *you* some things, all the things in this bag." She took the canvas tote from her shoulder. "I brought a surprise for you, too."

The little boy, becoming interested, seemed torn between going over to Sandy and starting to cry. "Something for me?"

"It's right in here." She patted the tote. "I'll show it to you once your daddy leaves for school. We don't want him to be late, do we?"

Bobby hesitated, then shook his head.

"I'll be back at four," Dr. Hudson said quickly, and giving the child's head a pat, picked up his briefcase and hurried out the door.

Bobby looked after him, but Sandy unzipped her bag, and at the sound, his attention swung to her. Keeping up a suspenseful show-and-tell, she emptied it item by item, explaining each one, from her hairbrush—he brushed his hair with it—to the book she planned to read for her literature class while he napped.

When Sandy had just about emptied her tote, he asked, "Where's my surprise?"

"Well, let's see if I can find it." She reached in and felt around. "Is it gone? No, here it is!" And she produced the plastic bottle of bubble solution and the bubble rings she'd brought for him.

Clearly, he'd never blown bubbles before. Outside, as he chased the transparent globes, his laughter floated through the air like the bubbles.

Then she heard, "Yoo-hoo!" She recognized Dr. Hudson's across-the-street neighbor Mrs. Gordon puffing up the driveway—overweight, with dyed brown hair and inquisitive, blue shoe-button eyes. When in high school, Sandy had often taken care of her two children.

The woman looked at the little boy playing so happily. "My, my, it looks as though everything worked out well, dear," she said. "Hi there, Bobby!"

"Hi," he replied, and he ran off into the yard, still blowing and chasing bubbles.

"Thank you again for providing a reference to Dr. Hudson for me," said Sandy.

"Well, I've been his neighbor for a long time, and I thought you'd be perfect. I told him how good you were with my children." Mrs. Gordon lowered her voice. "I also told him that your father had died recently and that it was your mother who taught his older son in fifth grade. What was that boy's name? You know that Dr. Hudson and his wife divorced about ten years ago, don't you? She got custody of the boy."

"Yes, Jeff was in my mother's class for part of a year, and yes, I knew Dr. Hudson and his wife divorced."

Mrs. Gordon glanced at Bobby, stepped closer to Sandy, and spoke in a lowered voice. "For the next few years after that, Dr. Hudson was a real playboy. He went out with so many different women, all good-looking, I must say. I used to see them over here sometimes, even on the weekends when the son visited. But then he married Glenda, and they had Bobby. They're gone a lot, of course—he's teaching and she's in grad school. Luckily, his wife's mother lives here in town to help out, though now she's had that knee surgery." The woman paused. "Doesn't it seem strange to you that Glenda will be gone for so much of the summer? I sometimes wonder if this marriage is breaking up, too."

"He told me, when I went for my interview, that he wanted her to go on a dig in Israel when she had the opportunity. She's doing research for her dissertation."

"He *wanted* her to go?" exclaimed Mrs. Gordon. "That seems even stranger to me. Maybe he looks forward to being free again."

"Oh, no—and he's not free. He's keeping Bobby." Sandy glanced at her phone. "It's almost ten o'clock— he'll want to watch the latest *Sesame Street* on television, and I need to straighten the house. Come on, time to go in," she called to the little boy. "See you later, Mrs. Gordon."

Much later, I hope, she thought. For much as she hated to admit it, the woman's gossip disturbed her.

In the house with Bobby contentedly watching television, she dusted the archeological artifacts and the framed pictures of Dr. Hudson and Glenda—a dark-haired, smooth-skinned young woman wearing horn-rimmed glasses. These pictures and the baby pictures of the little boy with his parents helped dismiss Mrs. Gordon's suspicions. Obviously, Dr. Hudson was happily married now. She gave Bobby his lunch, put him in for his nap, and made out a grocery list.

Then, reading her book on a chaise lounge on the screened porch at the side of the house, she heard a vehicle come speeding up the driveway. She stood up to look. It was an old, white SUV loaded with duffel bags, a backpack, a sleeping bag, a lamp, books. She went outside. Someone must have come to the wrong house.

****

As Sandy walked out to the driveway, a tanned, muscular young man in shorts and a white T-shirt got out of the SUV. He had a cleft in his chin, thick, dark, slightly curly hair that grew down past his ears, and the hard body of an athlete—or physical laborer.

"Excuse me," she said. "I think you've come to the wrong place."

"No, I haven't." His eyes blazed angry gold sparks as he looked her up and down. "*Dr. Hudson* didn't waste any time, did he? He always liked young, pretty ones, but your age? You do know he's married, don't you? That his wife is gone for the summer and he has a three-year-old son?"

She stared back at him, incredulous as she realized what he was thinking. "Of course I know all that. I'm here babysitting for his three-year-old son. I'm here Mondays, Wednesdays, and Fridays, nine to four."

"Come on," said the young man. "I may not be in close touch with my father, but I know Bobby stays with his grandmother while his mother is away."

My father? So he was Jeff Hudson. Yes, there was the resemblance to the tough fifth grader she remembered. He seemed now to feel as much antagonism toward her, and toward his father also, as he had toward those boys he fought on the playground all those years ago. Perhaps that tinge of sympathy she'd felt for him had been misplaced. She felt her own wave of anger.

"Well, you're enough out of touch with your father that you didn't know Bobby's grandmother had a knee replacement. She couldn't take care of him after all."

"Oh, is that it? Where is Bobby then?"

"He's taking a nap."

The antagonism in his expression began to fade. A slight flush spread across his cheekbones under the tan. "I'm sorry," he said after a moment. "I made a mistake."

"It wouldn't have happened if you'd let your father know you were coming."

"He said I could stay in his garage apartment if I needed a place. I texted him yesterday that I did want to—for a few weeks. He must not have seen it." He paused, concerned. "I really do apologize…I should leave, then drive back in and start all over again."

Sandy remembered Mrs. Gordon's description of Dr. Hudson's "playboy" phase. The wave of anger within her calmed, and she smiled—just a little. "That won't be necessary."

Jeff let out a breath. He smiled too—just a little. "Thanks." He turned and surveyed the upper story of the garage. "I need to check with my father. I don't have a key."

"Dr. Hudson is at school right now. You should call his office."

He produced a phone from his pocket and tapped a few times, then listened intently a minute before he spoke. "Hello," he said in a leave-a-message voice. "This is Jeff. Did you get my text? I do want to take you up on your offer of the apartment. I'm at your house now. Give me a call." He clicked off, then, and leaning back against his SUV, regarded Sandy again. "You look a little familiar."

"I'm Sandy Harris. I was two grades behind you at

Lumpkin Elementary. My mother was your teacher in fifth grade."

"Oh, Mrs. Harris." He ran a hand back over his hair. "What do you remember?"

How you made all the fifth-grade boys afraid of you. How you broke into the school and stole some money. How much my mother disliked you... And how when you bumped into me that day outside my mother's classroom, you kept me from falling.

"I don't remember much. Just that you used to get into fights on the playground."

"That's all?"

"Yes, that's all."

"Your mother always said I had 'poor impulse control.' You just saw it." Again, he smiled faintly. "I gave her a hard time that year."

"Do you still get in fights?"

He laughed at that. "I've found other outlets for my impulses."

What impulses do you have now? What other outlets?

"Where have you been all these years?"

"I lived with grandparents and my mother in Atlanta after my parents divorced. After high school, I went to Georgia Tech for three semesters. Then I took a break from school. For the past couple of years, I've worked in North Carolina on my uncle's farm."

"But you're at the University of Georgia now?"

"I've transferred to the College of Agriculture and Environmental Sciences. I'm taking classes this summer. Are you a UGA student?"

"I'll be in my third year this fall."

His phone let out some lively music. Jeff put it to

his ear. "Hi, Dad. You got my message? So I can stay in the apartment for a couple of weeks or so? Thanks a lot. What about a key? Okay, under the steps. I'll find it...Yes, I met her." He looked at Sandy. "My father wants to know how Bobby is doing."

When she took the phone from him, she felt on it the residual warmth from his hand. "Hello, Dr. Hudson. Bobby's doing great."

"I didn't know Jeff would be coming," he said. "I apologize for the intrusion."

"It was no intrusion. Bobby's taking a nap now."

"Good. I'll see you at four."

"Okay," said Sandy. "Bye." She handed the phone back to Jeff.

"Intrusion?"

"Oh, he just apologized because he hadn't told me you were coming."

"He shouldn't apologize—he didn't know." Jeff paused, withdrawing into his own thoughts for a moment.

"What is it?" asked Sandy.

"I just...I figured I wouldn't be intruding on anybody. I knew my father's wife wouldn't be here, that he'd spend a lot of time at his office, and Bobby would be at his grandmother's. I thought my father and I would just lead our separate lives. Now, I don't know. He'll be home on Tuesdays and Thursdays, and you'll be here the other days during the week."

"That's true."

"Well," said Jeff slowly, as if thinking aloud, "that shouldn't be a problem. I'll spend most of the time in my classes, studying in the library, working out at the Ramsey Center, swimming at the university pool." His tone changed. "My father told me where to find the key, so I can move this stuff in. Will that bother you now?"

"Oh, no," said Sandy. "But Bobby will wake up any minute."

"He's never seen me. I don't think he even knows about me. What will you tell him?"

"I don't know. What do you think?"

Jeff's brow furrowed.

"I'll keep Bobby inside. He won't need to meet you right away. Later, your father can introduce you and tell him you are his brother."

"His brother." Jeff shook his head. "I never felt I had a brother."

"You do now."

****

Jeff must have moved in quickly and then left, for his SUV was gone when Sandy next looked out. At four, when Dr. Hudson pulled into the driveway, Sandy was putting their snack dishes in the dishwasher. Bobby sat at the kitchen table with his crayons and paper, drawing.

When his father entered the kitchen, the little boy jumped up and ran over to him, holding up his picture. "Well, hello," said Dr. Hudson, putting his briefcase down and picking him up. "What's this?"

"A lion-dog," said Bobby, "part lion, part dog. And guess what, Daddy? Sandy and I blew bubbles."

"Everything went well," Sandy confirmed, brushing back a tendril of hair. "He was a good boy. Why don't you finish your picture, Bobby, and I'll talk to your daddy for a minute?"

"Okay."

Dr. Hudson set his little son back down, and he

went back to work scribbling on his picture. Sandy closed the dishwasher door. "I wondered if I could take Bobby to the university's outdoor pool Wednesday afternoon."

"Of course. He'd love that." He took out his wallet. "Here is his faculty dependent ID card so he can get in. There's an extra child car seat in the garage. If it's okay with you, I'll install it in your car for you this afternoon since you may be taking Bobby there and other places this summer. Oh, and one more thing." He turned from the scribbling child, his brow furrowed much like Jeff's, and spoke quietly. "I hope you won't mind that my older son will stay in the apartment over the garage for a few weeks this summer. Knowing him, he'll keep pretty much to himself."

"I'm sure there will be no problem."

****

Her mother called to her from the kitchen as Sandy entered the house. "How did your day go?" When she came to the kitchen, Mrs. Harris, in capris, T-shirt, and an apron, was at the kitchen counter snapping green beans for dinner.

"It went well. Bobby's a sweet, smart little boy. I'll have fun taking care of him." She paused, glancing over hesitantly at her mother. "And guess who showed up there today, of all people? Jeff Hudson."

"Jeff?" The woman's hands stopped moving. "What was *he* doing there?"

"He's taking summer classes at the university and staying in an apartment the Hudsons have over their garage."

"Dr. Hudson never told you he'd be staying there."

"It was last minute. Jeff won't be around much."

"That's good."

"I think he doesn't get along with his father."

"Why do you say that?"

"For one thing, he hasn't come to visit him here for the last few years. He said he's never met Bobby. He thinks Bobby doesn't even know about him." Sandy sat at the kitchen table. "Mrs. Gordon came by today. She told me Dr. Hudson was a real playboy after his wife left, that he dated a lot of different women."

"People certainly date after they are divorced. My sister—your aunt Mary—did."

Sandy had often heard the story of Aunt Mary's abusive first husband, how later she met her second, Uncle Tim, a warm, loving man. "I wonder why Dr. Hudson and his wife divorced."

"I don't know. Usually, one parent tells the story one way, the other tells it another. However it happened, they obviously had major problems in their marriage."

"Mom, I remember coming to your classroom one day after school. I saw you questioning Jeff about something. You seemed really angry and told me to wait outside in the hall. Do you remember what that was about?"

Mrs. Harris adjusted her glasses a little nervously and turned back to snapping beans. "It could have been about many things. He got in trouble all the time. Finally, when he broke into the school and stole that money, the city's juvenile courts got involved. The judge thought his parents' divorce would actually be a good thing for him. He talked the school into dropping the charges from the break-in and gave his mother and her parents joint custody." She turned again and looked sternly at her daughter. "Considering how Jeff behaved that year, he probably has not turned out well. You should keep your distance from him."

Chapter Three

Sandy could not help but look for Jeff's SUV when she arrived at the Hudson house on Wednesday morning, but it was gone. Inside, cleaning up the kitchen after Dr. Hudson left, she found no extra dishes in the dishwasher, no hint anywhere of Jeff's presence.

"Have you met Jeff?" she asked Bobby, who was playing on the kitchen floor with some little toy trucks.

The little boy looked up at her. "Who is Jeff?"

It's been two days and he has not met him. Sandy did not pursue the topic. While Bobby took his nap after lunch, she changed to her bathing suit—a turquoise one-piece with a V-neck—and added to her large tote two bottles of apple juice, crackers, a few pool toys, and an inflatable tube. When Bobby woke up, she helped him into his bathing suit, added his towel to her own, and drove him to the pool.

The water sparkled invitingly as they arrived. Sandy put her tote on a picnic table, spread out their towels beside the pool, took off Bobby's shirt and sneakers. "We'd better get some sunscreen on you."

"Can we go in the big pool?" the child asked as he endured her ministrations.

"I'll take you there in a few minutes. You play with your toys in the children's pool for a while first, okay?"

Bobby agreeably carried his bucket and plastic toys

over to the small, shallow pool reserved for children under six. There he struck up a conversation with two other little boys. Sandy watched them, then took off her beach wrap, applied sunscreen, and sat cross-legged nearby, occasionally leafing through a magazine she'd brought with her. Other people arrived. The families with small children, by unwritten consent, settled at her end of the pool; students settled at the other end. In one of the far lanes, she noted a young man doing laps.

"Sandy!" Bobby called to her after a while. "Can we go in the big pool now?"

"Sure, honey. You've been very good. I need to blow up your tube, though."

"I'll get it." The little boy scrambled out of the water and ran over to the picnic table. He took the flattened tube out of the bag and brought it to Sandy. She began blowing it up, as he stood at her side, bouncing up and down in eagerness.

Suddenly Sandy felt a cool, wet presence above her, and a few delicious drops of water fell on her sun-warmed shoulders. She looked up. Her heart skipped a beat. He must have been the swimmer she'd noticed in the lap lane.

"Jeff," she said. "Hi."

"Hi." He sat down on the deck on her other side, his body still streaming with water, a puddle forming around him. He indicated the tube in her hands. "I can finish blowing that up for you."

Sandy, still surprised as well as distracted by his muscular build, tried to recover herself. "Oh, thank you. Bobby, this is…Jeff." Deciding not to identify him further, she handed over the tube. "Jeff, this is Bobby."

Jeff looked closely at the little boy. "Hello there."

"Bobby, aren't you going say hello?"

"Hello," said Bobby dutifully, and he focused his attention on the tube as Jeff finished inflating it, then punched in the valve and handed it to him.

"Here you go. Let's see you try it out in that little pool."

Bobby grabbed it, about to run off, when Sandy caught his arm. "What do you say?"

"Thank you!" The little boy slipped the tube over his head to his waist, ran to the edge of the shallow pool, and jumped in.

"He's cute," said Jeff.

"I'm surprised you've never come to see him."

Jeff looked out over the expanse of the larger pool. "I never considered my father's new family any relation to me."

Sandy regarded him thoughtfully. "I see."

"Can we go to the big pool now?" Bobby called.

"All right, honey." She got to her feet. "I promised I'd take him. He's been waiting." She felt Jeff watching her as she went over to the child, took his hand, and walked with him to the pool's edge. Jumping in, she held out her arms, and he leaped to her, the tube still around his middle.

She was towing him toward the deep end when Jeff swam up beside them. "Hey, Bobby, want me to give you a ride on my shoulders?"

"Yes," exclaimed Bobby, no longer shy.

"Is that all right with you, Sandy?"

She nodded. Jeff ducked down under him and rose up, so that the little boy, tube and all, rode high above him. Sandy felt happy Jeff had joined them, though slightly anxious to see Bobby carried off. When she saw Jeff lift him up and toss him into the water, she started to go to them, but the child bobbed up laughing. "Again!" he said.

Jeff did toss him again—several times, then said, "How would you like to swim?" Bobby nodded eagerly, wiping water from his eyes. Jeff held him horizontally in the water and said, "Now kick your feet and move your arms like this." When he did so, Jeff took his arms out from under Bobby who, still with the tube around him, kicked and paddled off delightedly.

Jeff turned to Sandy. "He's taken right to it."

"You're a good teacher," Sandy said. Then she called, "Now come back to us, Bobby!"

"He should try it without the tube," Jeff commented, as the little boy turned and paddled toward them.

She held out her hands and drew Bobby to her. "Maybe another time."

"Where did Jeff go?" the little boy asked after a moment.

Looking around, Sandy did not see him. Suddenly, strong hands pulled her underwater. She reached down and, feeling Jeff's broad, slippery shoulders under her, held tight to them. Holding her ankles, he rose up out of the water with her on his shoulders as Bobby had been. The child laughed delightedly at the sight as, her wet hair streaming over her shoulders, Sandy gasped and coughed a little.

"Are you okay?" Jeff asked.

She laughed too. "I'm fine." She slid off into the water beside him. "But now it *is* time to get out."

They climbed the steps out of the pool and walked over to the spot where she had been sitting. She dried

Bobby, who was shivering a little, and wrapped him in his towel. She turned to Jeff. "I've brought some apple juice," she said, "if you'd like some."

"Sure."

Sandy poured the little boy a cup of juice from one of the small bottles she'd brought. While he sat on the deck beside the pool with the snacks, she and Jeff settled on the picnic table behind him. She handed Jeff a bottle of juice and took for herself the other now partially empty bottle. "Bobby had such a good time with you," she said. "I think you could really get him to start swimming."

"I've never done anything with little kids."

As if he'd heard, the child turned around, hooded in his towel. "Jeff, come swim with us next time!"

Jeff looked pleased, as if in spite of himself. "Maybe," he said. "Right now"—he glanced at the pool clock—"I need to go and do some reading for my classes. Summer sessions move fast."

Sandy saw that it was twenty until four. "We need to get back too." As they got off the table, she said, "Thanks for playing with Bobby."

"It was fun." Jeff raised a palm for a high five, and the child happily smacked it. "See you, buddy," he said.

Sandy watched as he walked toward the other end of the pool where he'd left his things. Then she turned and packed her tote. As she took Bobby's hand to leave, the two little boys he had been playing with waved at him. "They're your friends now, aren't they?" she said.

"Yes," Bobby replied. "They are brothers."

****

When Dr. Hudson arrived home a few minutes after four, Bobby ran to him, excited. "We went to the pool, and someone named Jeff swam with us. He let me jump off his shoulders like you do, Daddy!"

Dr. Hudson looked over at Sandy. "Jeff did that?"

"He was at the pool, too," she said.

"Well, I'm glad you had fun," Dr. Hudson said. "And you know what, Bobby? Jeff is going to be staying for the next few weeks in the apartment over our garage—up there, see?" He went to the kitchen door and pointed through the screen up at the second-story apartment.

"Why, Daddy?"

Dr. Hudson hesitated a moment, then said, "So he can take classes at my school this summer. Hey, it's time for the afternoon *Sesame Street*. I see Sandy's turned it on for you."

"Oh, good!" The little boy ran into the family room, and his father turned to Sandy. He looked uncomfortable. "You didn't tell him who Jeff was?"

"No."

"That's probably good. He wouldn't understand his—and my—relationship to Jeff right now." He paused, then seemed to decide to tell her more. "For years, Jeff and I haven't gotten along. After his mother and I divorced, he'd only visit me here by court order one weekend a month until he reached eighteen. Then he didn't even have to do that anymore. So he's never met Glenda or Bobby."

Sandy realized what he was saying was painful, but he obviously wanted to explain the situation to her. Not knowing what to say, she just nodded.

"I wish we could be on better terms," Dr. Hudson went on. "I didn't spend much time with Jeff when he was young. I hope to do better by Bobby…I'm glad Jeff played with him at the pool. And surprised."

"They really had a good time together."

"Maybe this summer, while he's here for an extended period of time, things can change between Jeff and me. I've tried to make it up to him before, but it's been very difficult. Well, this does not concern you!" He laughed a little. "I wanted to ask you—I've been invited to a dinner Friday night. Could you extend your hours and spend Friday evening here?"

"I'd be glad to."

"Good. Well, just plan on staying past the usual time on Friday then—fix a supper and put Bobby to bed by eight. I won't be late."

****

Jeff pulled off his T-shirt and khakis, then lay down on the foldout couch he used as a bed. He'd tossed his belongings haphazardly around the one-room apartment. A small bathroom with a shower had been built at the end of the room; a counter separated the kitchen area on the side, and beside it, a small wooden table and two chairs provided a place to eat. He'd bought some cold cereal, a few frozen dinners that barely fit in the refrigerator's little freezer, milk, a six-pack of beer. The air conditioner in the window rumbled on low.

He had reading to do for both of his courses, which had the rather unwieldy names *Analytical and Computational Tools for Applied Economics* and *Environmental Law and Governmental Regulation*. He reached for the environmental law textbook, propped himself up on a pillow, and opened it. He'd have to hustle to keep up. He wanted to get good grades, get his courses over with, maybe finish his degree in less than two years. Being here this summer gave him a head start and so far, it hadn't been as bad in Athens as he'd thought it would be. It seemed far enough away from Atlanta after all.

Probably he'd been paranoid to think of the drug supplier he'd worked with finding him here and wanting him to deal again. He liked his classes. And what a surprise to find this beautiful girl babysitting for his father. That initial mix-up when he drove in—how embarrassing! But apparently, she'd forgiven him. When he'd seen her that afternoon at the pool—that long blonde hair, her bare shoulders gleaming with sunscreen oil—he couldn't stop himself from approaching her; and when she looked up at him, he was startled by the vivid blue of her eyes.

As for Bobby, the child's dark hair and sturdy little body reminded him of the snapshots of himself as a young kid that his mother still kept in a bulging photo album. He'd felt a strange urge to be to Bobby what he wished his father had been to him.

Being with the two of them that afternoon at the pool had seemed so natural. He hadn't been with young children much, and not with a girl for a long time. Still, he reminded himself, he wanted to keep his distance from his father, and thus Bobby. As for Sandy, her mother's memories of him would not be good ones. If by any wild chance she'd also somehow heard of his arrest in Atlanta...No, the strict Mrs. Harris he remembered would not approve of her daughter associating with him.

His phone played some music and he answered. A bright female voice came through. "Hi, Jeff. It's Sheila."

Of course he knew who it was. Sheila Odashion had been in middle and high school with him—a tall, statuesque girl who reminded him of an Egyptian princess. They had dated pretty furiously for a while their sophomore year. Although they were in the same grade, she was one year older than he, and many years more experienced. She'd had numerous other male interests and after a while, moved on—and so had he. It had been a shock when, as he was leaving his first class that day, he heard a female voice exclaim, "Jeff Hudson!" and it was Sheila—four years older now, and as sexy as ever.

"What are you doing here?" she'd asked.

"I'm getting a degree in CAES," he said. "What about you?"

"I'm majoring in landscape architecture. It's a five-year program, and I'm taking this course as an elective. You look great, Jeff. We must get together for old time's sake."

"Yeah, it's been a while." She, at least, did not seem to know of his more recent past at Tech. Maybe she wouldn't have minded anyway.

"What's your cell number? I'll text you mine."

He could only oblige, then had to rush off to his next class. And now she was calling him.

"There's a good movie at the student union tomorrow night," she was saying. "Why don't we go together? We can have some drinks afterward. And catch up." Her voice lowered with unmistakable meaning. "I have never forgotten you."

Jeff shifted uneasily on the bed. He wasn't ready to get involved in a hookup so soon. Sheila had tried to get back together with him their senior year in high school too, but he'd evaded her then. Yes, he'd go to the movie with her now for old time's sake, but he was pretty sure that was all he wanted to do.

****

That evening, Sandy found herself reliving her chance encounter with Jeff at the pool—and thinking of how handsome he was and how good he'd been with Bobby. This Jeff was so different from the budding criminal her mother and Bill said he'd been in fifth grade. *But this afternoon was just a chance meeting. I probably won't see him again.*

When she heard her phone buzz shortly after dinner, Bill's name came up on the screen. She answered, turning away from her mother. "Hi."

"A foreign film is playing at the university student union tomorrow."

"I've read about that movie. It sounds interesting."

"So shall I pick you up at seven-thirty?"

"Okay."

"Good. See you then."

****

Sandy spent Thursday morning in her Victorian novels class and the afternoon catching up on the homework. The students were to participate in written online conversations about Mary Shelly's *Frankenstein,* the novel they were currently reading. Sitting in a big leather chair in the study lounge at the student learning center, she enjoyed looking at her classmates' comments on her laptop and adding some of her own. She wrote that she felt sorry for Frankenstein's monster, all alone watching the happy family living near his hiding place, afraid to show himself because they would be so horrified by his appearance.

Back at home late that afternoon, she ate a light supper with her mother, then showered and changed to pencil-slim white jeans and a pink scoop-necked tank top, preparing for the movie with Bill—it would be a more traditional date now. On the dot, he rang the bell. She answered the door. There he stood, tall, slim, and fresh, with his close-clipped blond hair and pale, green eyes, looking like a golf shirt model in a television commercial.

"Hi," he said. "Where's your mother? I'd like to say hello."

"In the backyard. Come on." She led him through the house, out into the sunroom, and down the steps to the terrace where her mother sat in a deck chair with her after-dinner iced tea and a book.

"Bill!" She stood up and once again hugged him warmly. "Can you sit down and talk a while?"

"The movie starts at eight, Mom," Sandy said.

"Would you like to come along with us?" Bill asked.

"Oh no, thank you. But I do want you to come here for dinner soon."

"I'd like that." Sandy and Bill said goodbye to her then and went around the side of the house to his car, parked at the curb. As he drove the few blocks to the university, he looked over at her. "You look as if you'd been on a beach vacation."

"I took Bobby to the university pool yesterday."

"While I was running around getting fertilizer spreaders and fence posts for customers at the store and giving advice about plants."

"So you miss Chapel Hill? And Spain?"

He laughed a little guiltily and touched her hand.

43

"There are advantages to being here, too."

He turned into a student parking lot, open to the public in evening hours. They strolled over the wide sidewalks under arching branches of oak trees to the student union and there joined the line at the ticket window. As Sandy perused the people ahead of them, she suddenly drew in her breath. Way up ahead, almost at the ticket window, stood Jeff Hudson, a dark-haired girl with a slightly hooked nose that was somehow exotic pressing close to his side. Sandy felt stunned that he had a date. He had just gotten to Athens three days ago.

"What's the matter?" Bill asked.

"I thought I saw someone I knew up there at the front of the line, but I was wrong." She did not want to identify Jeff, especially knowing Bill's hostility toward him.

Seated in the theater a few minutes later though, she could not help but try to locate him and the girl. She spotted them, sitting farther back on one side of the theater, Jeff's arm across the back of her seat. Sandy turned around quickly, but it was too late. She knew he'd seen her. He'd looked right at her.

She kept her eyes ahead after that, relieved when the movie started. But as she and Bill watched the plot unravel and exchanged occasional whispered comments, she remained aware of Jeff behind her with that dark-haired girl.

Bill wanted to stay for the credits, and so by the time they left, Jeff and the girl had disappeared. "I know you have to work tomorrow, but do you have time for a seltzer?"

"I do," she said. But the waiting line at the drink

counter was long.

"I'll get us cans out of this machine," Bill said. "We can drink them outside. What's your preference?" He read "Cucumber Ginger, Rosemary Mint, Cinnamon Grapefruit…" He glanced at her. "Original Virgin."

"Rosemary Mint," she replied quickly.

Bill shoved in change, made the selections, and the cans dropped down. He picked them up and handed her the Rosemary Mint.

Outside, they walked to a nearby bench. The night air was soft, and in the sky, a crescent moon was rising. She and Bill sat sipping their drinks and discussing the movie. And then he leaned close to her, put his hand behind her head, and kissed her gently, not on the cheek like a brother, but on the lips. She did not move away. But his kiss felt like a sort of experiment. She wondered fleetingly if his mother was pressuring him to pursue her romantically, as her own mother was pressuring her.

Bill drew away. "I guess we'd better go." He picked up their seltzer cans and dropped them into a recycling bin as they walked back to his car. "I'm sorry I'll be gone this weekend. I did promise Dad I'd play with him in the tournament. We're meeting Frank Golden, a friend of mine at The University of North Carolina. He's from Atlanta and he's playing in the tournament, too."

"I know you'll have a good time. I'm going to babysit for Bobby Friday night anyway."

"I'll see you on Sunday after I get back."

****

On Friday morning, Sandy returned to the Hudson house, her bathing suit packed, planning to take Bobby to the pool in the afternoon. Bobby asked her at once,

45

"Will we go to the pool today? Will Jeff be there?"

"Haven't you seen Jeff here?"

The child shook his head. "But I saw his big car." The parking area by the garage was empty now. Sandy thought, Jeff is keeping his word about not bothering anybody here. But maybe he will be at the pool again this afternoon.

She managed to get Bobby up from his nap so they could get there about the same time as they had on Wednesday. Sitting on her towel, watching Bobby in the children's pool, she looked out at the lap lanes, but now only a middle-aged woman was swimming. Bobby seemed to read her thoughts. Looking over at the woman also, he asked, "Will Jeff come today?"

"I don't know, honey. He said he might come, but he may be busy with his classes." She stood up. "Come on, I'll take you to the big pool."

"I want to jump off Jeff's shoulders again."

"You can jump off mine."

"His shoulders are bigger and higher."

"I can throw you into the water just as well," said Sandy. "And—he may come later." She did her best to keep Bobby happy, but he'd been spoiled by his time with Jeff. As the hands of the clock hands crept around toward four, Jeff still had not come. Hiding her own disappointment, she poured apple juice for Bobby. She had jinxed it, she thought, by bringing an extra bottle this time. Finally, she began repacking their things. "Bobby, we need to go home."

To her surprise, Bobby started to cry. "Jeff didn't come."

"He only said *maybe*," she told him. "We will see him another time. How about we stop at the drug store on the way home and get you an ice cream cone?" Bobby shook his head. "What kind do you like?" she persisted. "Let me guess. Vanilla?"

Bobby looked at her now and shook his head a different way. "Chocolate."

At the drugstore, as the child eagerly watched the boy behind the counter scoop ice cream out of the carton, she thought, *how nice to be three years old and comforted by a chocolate cone.* "On second thought, make that two cones."

****

After their supper at Dr. Hudson's kitchen table, Sandy took Bobby for a walk around the neighborhood, or rather, she walked while he rode his tricycle. Just as they were returning to the house, Bobby spotted Jeff's big white SUV turning into the Hudson driveway. "Look, there he is!"

"Yes," said Sandy, surprised at the breathlessness of her own voice, the thumping of her heart. And then she saw that with him was the dark-haired girl.

Jeff's car stopped in the parking area by the garage apartment, and he and the girl got out. Sandy heard their laughter as they went up the stairs to the apartment.

"Jeff!" Bobby called, leaning forward to pedal fast up the driveway.

"Shhh!" Embarrassed, Sandy grabbed the handlebars of the tricycle to stop him. "Don't you see he has company?"

Bobby, struggling to get free as Jeff and the girl disappeared inside, began to cry with frustration. Sandy hurried him into the house and tried to comfort him with "Maybe you'll see him tomorrow."

47

But she was afraid this, too, would give him a false hope. She changed Bobby into his pajamas but had to rock him to sleep. She looked down at his flushed, tear-stained face. *Poor little boy*, she thought. *Your mother has to be gone for most of the summer, your grandmother can't take care of you, and your brother appears and plays with you once and gets you to like him—then abandons you. And you don't even know he is your brother*. She felt abandoned herself.

After putting the sleeping child into his bed, she went back to the living room and picked up *Frankenstein*, but it was hard for her to concentrate. *I wonder if I should have let Bobby catch Jeff. Was it my own hurt pride—and maybe jealousy—that made me hold him back?* She resolved to make it up to Bobby. She would speak to Jeff about how much the child wanted to see him, remind him Bobby was his brother.

The house felt stuffy. Sandy opened the French doors onto the screened porch to let in the cool night air. Then she sat on the couch again to read, but in the aftermath of the warm afternoon and the pool, she slumped sideways and dozed. She wasn't sure how long she'd been asleep, but voices and the sound of footsteps coming down the garage apartment stairs roused her. Then car doors slammed, an engine growled, and through the window, she saw Jeff's SUV backing out of the driveway.

Sandy looked at her phone. It was eleven o'clock. At least the girl had not spent the night with Jeff. But maybe they were going back to wherever she lived. She understood anew how Frankenstein's monster had felt watching the happy family from his hiding place.

Sandy turned the television on to the weather

48

channel. The weather map was showing sun and mild temperatures for the next day when she heard Jeff's Durango turning back into the driveway. *He had not stayed with the girl!* And here was her chance to tell him about Bobby. She switched off the television and went out to the screened porch at the side of the house. Jeff had parked and gotten out of the SUV. When she turned on the porch light, he looked over. She motioned to him.

He walked to the side of the porch and looked up at her, his hands in his pockets. The light reflected dark gold in his eyes. "I didn't know you were here tonight."

Chapter Four

From her upper level on the porch, Sandy looked through the screen at Jeff. "I'm babysitting while your father is out at a dinner. Can I talk to you for a minute?"

"Sure," he said.

She thought his tone sounded a little guarded, but she unhooked the lock on the screen door. "You'd better come in." He came up the steps and through the door. "I wanted to talk to you about Bobby."

Jeff looked surprised. "What about him?"

"He missed you today when I took him to the pool. He kept asking when you would come. And tonight, he was so excited when he saw you drive in, but I didn't let him go to you. I thought you wouldn't want to be interrupted while you were…with someone. Then he started to cry. I felt terrible. I didn't know if I'd done the right thing. Of course, he doesn't know you're his brother, but he liked you so much and was so disappointed…"

"Shhh," Jeff said. "You're making me feel bad." She remained quiet then, just looking at him. He sat down sideways on the lounge chair, looking deep in thought. Then he seemed to decide. He looked up. "I have an idea. How about you and I take Bobby canoeing tomorrow?"

"Canoeing?" She felt her expression change, the

same way Bobby's had that afternoon after she'd handed him the chocolate ice cream cone. "But what about—" She gestured toward the apartment. "—your friend?"

"I could ask you the same thing—about the guy you were with at the movie last night."

"Oh, he's—just someone from high school."

"And Sheila's someone *I* went to high school with. She's in the economics course I'm taking this summer. We worked on an assignment tonight. My apartment's a lot quieter place to work than hers."

Sandy processed this a moment, then, relieved and happy, nodded. "Bobby would love canoeing with you. Would it be safe for him?"

"Sure. I know a part of the Oconee River between here and Greensboro that has a nice, gentle current— and great scenery. We'd put a life preserver on him, of course. Do you paddle?"

"Oh, yes." Then she had a thought. "Would your father let him go?" When Jeff hesitated, she answered for him. "I know he'd be glad for you to do things with Bobby. I think, since it's a safe part of the river and I'm going too, he'll give his permission."

"What about *your* parents?"

Sandy lowered her gaze. "My father died two months ago. He seemed fine and then—he had a heart attack. That's why I stayed home this summer—to be with my mother."

"I'm sorry," Jeff said. He paused. "Maybe you shouldn't go away all day Saturday, then."

Remembering her mother's warning that she should keep her distance from Jeff, she hesitated.

He stood and turned to go. "Maybe another time."

"No, wait." She would not lose this opportunity. "My mother will be fine. She goes out to lunch every Saturday with a group of women friends." She would tell her mother the truth: that Jeff needed her with them to establish his relationship with Bobby. "She'll want me to go," she finished, trying to sound confident.

Jeff absorbed this for a moment. "You're sure?" She nodded. "Then if it's okay with my father, I'll pick you up around eight tomorrow morning. Could you bring a picnic lunch?"

"Of course."

They heard the sound of Dr. Hudson's car turning into the driveway. "We can ask him about the canoe trip now," said Jeff.

Seeing them, Dr. Hudson came to the lighted porch and entered. His evening out seemed to have put him in a mellow mood. "Well," he said, eyeing Jeff. "I'm surprised to see you here."

Jeff extended his hand formally. "Sorry I haven't gotten to thank you before now for letting me stay in the apartment."

Dr. Hudson shook Jeff's hand. "Does it suit you?"

"It's great."

"Glad to hear it."

"I'd like to take Sandy and Bobby canoeing on the Oconee tomorrow, a safe part between here and Greensboro. I'd get to know him better, and with Sandy along, he should be fine."

"He sounded happy when he told me about playing with you at the pool Wednesday," said Dr. Hudson.

"He *was* happy," Sandy interjected. "I think he'd love canoeing with Jeff."

"In that case…I've wanted you to get to know

Bobby, and it's good that Sandy will go along. I have a graduate student's dissertation to read. I could do that while you are gone and then be free all day Sunday to be with Bobby. All right then." He laid a hand on Jeff's shoulder. "I do appreciate this."

Sandy saw Jeff tense slightly. "We'll leave here tomorrow morning about a quarter to eight. I'll come to the house and pick him up."

Dr. Hudson removed his hand. "I'll have him ready. We can put the child seat from my car into your SUV. Oh, and Sandy, here's your check." He reached for his wallet and extracted the oblong piece of paper.

"Thank you. I'll get my bag." Glad that everything was working out, Sandy went to the living room and returned with her tote over her shoulder. "Goodnight, Dr. Hudson."

Jeff began following Sandy out the porch door. "Why don't you stay here for a few minutes?" Dr. Hudson asked him. "We can talk."

"Another time," said Jeff. "I'll walk Sandy to her car." He gave a slight wave and closed the screen door behind him.

****

Late that night, Jeff lay on his couch-bed in the dark, unable to sleep. He'd told Sheila when he brought her home that he wanted just to be friends, and she'd seemed to accept that. "All right," she'd said. But as she leaned in to kiss him goodnight, he saw an added message in her dark eyes: "All right...for now."

Sheila, however, was not the reason he could not sleep.

Damn. I've broken my rule about staying away from Bobby because of my father—and about staying

53

away from Sandy because of her mother.
****

Sandy tiptoed into her house and saw the light on in what they called the family room, with its comfortable couch and chairs and the big, flat-screened television. She found her mother there in bathrobe and slippers, watching the late news. Mrs. Harris looked up as Sandy entered and clicked off the television. "Hi, honey," she said sleepily. "You've had a long day."

"Yes." Sandy sat on the footstool by her mother's chair.

Her mother studied her. "You don't seem tired. You seem—rather bright-eyed and excited. Is there a reason?"

"Jeff Hudson wants to take Bobby and me canoeing tomorrow. I knew you were going to lunch with your friends, so I said I'd go. I'm supposed to bring a picnic."

Her mother closed her book. Two parallel lines of worry appeared between her eyes. "How have you gotten to know Jeff? I thought you said he wasn't going to be around much."

Oh dear, I was afraid of this. I'll have to convince her this will be all right.

"We saw him at the university pool, and he and Bobby got along really well. Jeff thought taking Bobby canoeing tomorrow would be a chance for them to get to know each other better. They are brothers, after all. But someone else needs to go along with them. Dr. Hudson can't go—he has a dissertation to read. And since Bobby is used to me now…"

"I told you—I don't think it's a good idea for you to get involved with Jeff."

"This doesn't mean I'm *involved* with him. Anyway, a lot of time has passed. Jeff isn't the same as he was in your fifth grade."

"How do you know that? There's a saying, 'The child is father of the man.' The man hides his nature better than the child. And going on this canoe trip isn't part of your job."

"No. But Dr. Hudson wants me to go with them."

Sandy's mother's face still registered disapproval. "And you've already agreed to go?"

"Yes." Sandy reached over and patted her hand. "I promise it will be fine, Mom. And it's for a good cause. Would you mind if I made sandwiches for the picnic out of that chicken salad in the refrigerator?"

"At least you asked me about *that*." Mrs. Harris stood up and with an abrupt motion, snapped out the light she had been reading by. Then she looked down at her daughter. "I'm sorry, honey, it's just that I worry about you being with that boy. But I suppose, this one time, since the child will be with you and Dr. Hudson wants you to go…Okay, you can use the chicken salad for your sandwiches." She paused. "You aren't forgetting about Bill, are you?"

Sandy turned away. "He's away at a golf tournament with his father."

****

She was up early the next morning to make the chicken salad sandwiches plus a peanut butter and jelly for Bobby. She put them in the family cooler with frozen gel packs, then added some grapes and a few of her mother's homemade chocolate chip cookies from the freezer. Finally, she put lemonade in a large thermos and in her tote some plastic bottles of frozen water that would thaw on the way but stay cold. Finished with the picnic preparations, she took a shower and put on her bathing suit, then shorts and a navy blue and white striped T-shirt. Finally, she packed sunscreen, a sun hat, and tissues in her tote bag, and two rolled-up towels, one for Bobby in case Jeff or Dr. Hudson forgot.

A few minutes after eight, Jeff's SUV pulled up to the curb in front of her house with Bobby in a car seat in the back seat. Her mother, in the kitchen, called to her, "I think Jeff's here." Now would come the meeting Sandy dreaded.

As she came out on the front porch carrying the cooler and thermos, Jeff was on his way up the walk, wearing swim trunks, a T-shirt, and a baseball cap. He looked very athletic. "Here, I'll take those," he said.

Sandy handed them over, stepped back into the hall to get her tote, and walked to the SUV as Jeff was putting the cooler and thermos into the back.

"Sandy!" Bobby called from the car.

"Hi, honey!" She waved at him, then said quietly to Jeff, "My mother will be coming out to see you."

He put her tote beside the cooler and closed the back and met her eyes. "I thought she would."

As if on cue, her mother came out of the house. "Hello, Jeff," she said, scrutinizing him as she came down the walk. "It's been a long time."

"Hello, Mrs. Harris. Yes, over ten years."

"I have to say, I always wondered what happened to you."

"I'm doing all right." He smiled a little as he and Mrs. Harris briefly shook hands. "Believe it or not."

"Sandy said you'd gone to Georgia Tech."

"Yes, for a couple of years."

"Mom, come see Bobby," Sandy said, bringing her mother over to the SUV's back window.

After looking in, Mrs. Harris said, "Hello, Bobby."

The child, suddenly shy, stared at her curiously. "Hi," he almost whispered.

"We'd better get going, Mom. Have fun at your lunch." Sandy gave her mother a quick kiss. She and Jeff got in the front seat and buckled their seat belts. Mrs. Harris leaned over and looked in through the open window at Jeff. Her tone was curt. "What time shall I expect you back?"

"About dark, I think," he replied.

"That's a long day," her mother said. There was an uncomfortable pause. Then she said, "Be careful."

Jeff turned on the ignition. "Yes, ma'am, I will."

"I'll be watching for you at dark," her mother called out, a note of warning, Sandy thought, in her voice. The woman straightened and stepped back.

Jeff pulled away from the curb. Struck by a pang of guilt, Sandy called, "Love you, Mom. See you tonight."

As they drove down the street, she heard Jeff let out a breath. She looked over at him. "That wasn't as bad as it could have been."

"It was fine."

Sandy relaxed. "It's going to be a beautiful day."

They didn't know that as Mrs. Harris walked briskly back to the house, she was resolving to do some research on the computer. She wanted to find out anything she could about this older Jeff Hudson. He was too good-looking—and Sandy too impressionable. The incorrigible boy she'd had in her fifth-grade class, the one she'd thought herself rid of forever, obviously could now mean a different kind of trouble.

****

Jeff stopped to rent the life jackets and canoe at River Rentals, on the Oconee where it ran through Athens on its way south to join the Ocmulgee and Altamaha Rivers, then ultimately the ocean. With a clerk's help, he hoisted the canoe to the top of the car, protected with a canvas tarp. After he'd tightened the heavy straps fastening it, they headed down Route 15 toward the Oconee National Forest, where Jeff said they'd launch the canoe. After about half an hour, they reached the entrance. A rocky road down a steep incline led to the river. The SUV swayed as Jeff maneuvered to avoid the biggest rocks and ruts. "Hold on," he said.

"Wow!" Bobby squealed in delight.

"How did you know about this place?" asked Sandy, steadying herself against the car door.

"My uncle hunts back here. I like canoeing in deserted areas like this—you get to see more wildlife." At the end of the road, Jeff braked and turned off the ignition.

Sandy looked through the windshield to see a broad expanse of flowing water glittering in the sun. Trees along the edge, their roots exposed by erosion, leaned out over the riverbed, making a leafy archway. "This is amazing!" she exclaimed.

"Come on, I'll need your help with the canoe, and then we'll be on our way," said Jeff. "Bobby, you can get out and watch if you promise to stay back."

"I promise," he said.

Jeff unbuckled the straps securing the canoe; then Sandy helped him slide it off the top of the car. After it was on the ground, she applied sunscreen to herself and

Bobby. When Jeff loaded the canoe with a blanket, his backpack, the cooler, thermos, and Sandy's bag, she handed him the sunscreen and he applied it to himself. Then he slid the canoe, prow first, partway into the water. He put the child-sized life preserver on Bobby and threw the required two adult ones into the canoe.

"Okay," he said, "time to get on board."

Sandy adjusted her sun hat, climbed into the front of the canoe, and sitting on the seat, picked up the paddle there. Jeff put Bobby in the middle, seated on the folded blanket on the bottom. Then he pushed off the canoe, jumped in, and settled in the stern to steer.

Wildflowers filled the banks along the river, so they looked almost like a garden—Queen Anne's lace, fire pinks, wild phlox, daisies and black-eyed Susans. On the water, a kingfisher darted after a fish, and to Bobby's joy, they saw the dark streak of an otter swimming underwater. Perhaps best of all, as they rounded one curve, they came upon a doe and two fawns on the bank drinking from the river. They raised their heads as the canoe silently moved closer—then they turned and loped into the woods, flicking the white undersides of their tails.

When the sun was high overhead, Jeff had them stop on a grassy knoll for their picnic. He spread out the blanket, and Sandy, sitting cross-legged between him and Bobby, took out the sandwiches, cookies, and drinks and distributed them. "Do you want chicken salad or peanut butter and jelly?" she asked Bobby.

"Peanut butter and jelly!" he crowed—as she had expected.

After they ate, Bobby went to play at the nearby river's edge as Sandy repacked the food. Jeff stretched out beside her, keeping an eye on Bobby. "This is so wonderful," she said. "I never knew the river was here, so near the highway."

"Not many people know this stretch of the Oconee. Hunters do come here in the fall during duck and deer season, but during the rest of the year, it's pretty isolated. Which is the way I like it."

"And there are no whitewater rapids—which is the way I like it."

Jeff laughed and reaching over, touched her hand. "I'll give you some advanced paddling lessons sometime, if you want, but in kayaks. Rapids can be fun—like a carnival ride."

Sandy felt a little thrill. It sounded as though he wanted to see her again, in spite of that dark-haired girl. She imagined them shooting down rapids in kayaks side by side. "I'd like that," she said.

"Come play with me," Bobby called out to them, breaking the spell.

Jeff stood up. "I think I'll take him in the water."

"I'll come, too."

"And then I'd like to go just a little farther before turning back. I have something I want to show you."

"Will we have time?"

"Plenty of time."

Jeff took off his cap and tossed it onto the blanket, stripped off his T-shirt, and ran down to the river's edge. Sandy got out of her shorts and T-shirt and followed. Bobby was already in the shallow part of water, floating happily in his life preserver, Jeff at his side. "Watch those rocks in the shallow part," he warned her as she approached. "They're slippery." He stepped close to the edge and held out his hand to help her in. As she reached for it, she did, in fact, slip on a slimy rock and fell against him. He picked her up and holding her, stood there a moment, then turned and carried her out to deeper water. "You can swim here," he said, releasing her.

She was sorry he had to let her go.

After playing and swimming in the water awhile, Jeff and Bobby built a little dam on the edge of the bank while Sandy sat beside them, handing them stones and twigs for the project. But before long, Jeff said they had better start again. He and Sandy repacked the canoe, resumed their positions with Bobby in the middle, and paddled on.

"What I want to show you," said Jeff, "is a ruined nineteenth-century mill I found last year when I was here with my uncle. I did a little research. The mill was called Scull Shoals. It's a ghost town now."

"What's a mill?" asked Bobby.

"In this case, a place where the early settlers would bring their grain—corn and wheat—to be ground up for flour," said Jeff. "They dammed the river so the water flow could move a big grinding wheel." In a few minutes, Jeff said, "The mill's right around this curve, on the right."

Soon moss-covered brick walls with arched doorways came into view. Jeff steered close to them and then through one of the arches into the wet darkness under the building. They saw the remains of a water wheel and a large millstone with a hole in the middle.

Bobby gripped the sides of the canoe. "I'm scared!"

"There's nothing to be afraid of," said Jeff, but he

soon paddled the canoe out into the sunshine again. Sandy turned and looked at Jeff with a silent thank you. She sensed they felt the same about this abandoned mill: it was a time capsule revealing an era so different from their own.

"Going upstream will be slower," Jeff told Sandy after a few minutes. "This current isn't very strong, but we'll have to paddle a little harder. Are you okay?"

"I'm fine," said Sandy. But he was right—it took more effort to move the canoe along.

Presently, Jeff asked, "Is anyone getting hungry?"

"Me!" Bobby yelled.

"We ate the sandwiches and cookies," Sandy said.

"I'd added something to your cooler. Take a look."

Sandy laid down her paddle and lifted the cooler lid. Down in the bottom, under the remains of their picnic, she saw a plastic grocery bag she hadn't noticed before. Inside, she saw a package of hot dogs, another of buns, and a few little envelopes of mustard. "You brought matches and plan to roast these?" she asked.

"Absolutely right," replied Jeff.

A few minutes later, they stopped on another riverbank. Jeff gathered some sticks, built a little pyramid of them, and started a fire. Bobby watched the process with interest, and when Jeff gave him a hot dog on a stick to roast, he was delighted. Sandy, standing nearby, noted the sun low in the west. She thought of her mother and stepped to his side. "Will we get back to the car by dark?"

"Sure." He paused. "Don't you trust me?"

Realizing the question suggested more than just the logistics of a canoe trip, she hesitated. Then she said, "Of course I trust you!"

They stood there a moment facing each other. Then, back to business, he handed her T-shirt to her. "Here, it's getting cooler." He put Bobby's shirt on him as well, and his own. He gave Sandy a stick and hot dog, and then squatted by the fire beside her as they blackened their hot dogs over the flames. Their little supper tasted delicious.

When they'd eaten, Jeff put out the fire. They repacked and were about to get in the canoe when he said, "Wait a minute." He reached into the side pocket of his backpack and brought out a plastic tube of mosquito repellent. "Come here, Bobby, we better put some of this on you," he said, and he rubbed the cream onto Bobby's arms and legs. Then he turned to Sandy. "Now you, lady," and he rubbed the cream onto her arms and legs as impersonally, it seemed, as he had onto Bobby's. Yet she felt very aware of his hands upon her.

When they were back in the canoe, Jeff said, "We'll have a sunset." He was right. As they paddled, the sky became stained a bright pink, with pink shimmers reflecting on the water. Fireflies blinked in the woods, and a frog chorus peeped around them.

It was deep dusk when they returned to the spot where they had launched. Sandy strapped Bobby into his car seat. Then she and Jeff lifted the canoe back on the SUV and tightened the straps that held it. Soon they were bouncing up the rocky hill to the highway.

As they drove back to Athens, with the headlights of oncoming cars piercing the darkness and Bobby asleep in his child seat behind them, Sandy looked over at Jeff's profile. A wave of affection washed through her. Yes, she did trust him. Whatever became of their relationship, she would always remember the beauty of the river—and those brief moments in the water when he held her against his chest, and later when, with warm, strong hands, he rubbed lotion onto her skin.

Chapter Five

The next morning, Sandy slowly came to consciousness from a deep sleep. Opening her eyes, she smiled and stretched, enjoying even the soreness in her arms because it brought back the memory of the day before. Snuggling back down, she closed her eyes again and saw images of the preceding day with Jeff and Bobby—paddling the canoe, eating sandwiches on the grass, swimming in the river. Maybe when she was married, she and her husband and children would have times like that together.

The images suddenly dissipated as she remembered her mother's words: *I don't think it's a good idea for you to get involved with Jeff.*

Her mother had never before disapproved of anyone she'd dated. In high school, besides Bill, she'd gone out occasionally with boys she knew from her extracurricular activities—the swim team, the photography club, the school newspaper—but she'd never had a steady boyfriend. During her relationship with John, she wasn't living at home, so her mother wasn't there to supervise or worry.

I suppose Mom feels so distrustful of Jeff because of the way he was in fifth grade. Maybe, too, now that I'm old enough for a serious relationship, she thinks of her younger sister who, at about my age, eloped with someone she barely knew who turned out to be abusive.

Sandy thrust aside those thoughts and the shadows of doubt they evoked. Instead, she returned to the sweet memories of the day before. She replayed in her mind how Jeff had driven her home, left the car idling as Bobby continued to sleep, and turned to her. "Thank you for coming."

"Thank you for taking me," she replied—all she could think of to say.

"I'll see you soon." Then he got out of the car, taking care so as not to wake Bobby and carried the cooler to the door while Sandy followed with the thermos and her tote. Her mother met them at the door and took the cooler. Jeff then hurried to the car to take Bobby home.

I'll see you soon.

When is soon? Sandy had never felt this way about a boy before, even John. This tingly sense of magic was wonderful, if a little frightening. She reached for her phone and checked her messages. Nothing from Jeff. Surely, he did not mean this soon. And come to think of it, he did not even have her cell phone number.

A knock came on her door, and Mrs. Harris poked her head in. "Are you going to church with me?"

"What time is it?"

"Nine o'clock. I have breakfast ready."

"Great." After yesterday, Sandy felt she owed her. She pulled on her robe and followed her mother down the stairs.

"I've made a fruit compote and waffles."

"Sounds delicious."

As Mrs. Harris served her daughter's plate, she said, "How was your picnic?"

"Oh, Mom, it was wonderful! The river was beautiful. We saw flowers and wildlife and an old mill. Bobby loved it."

"I'm glad he did." Mrs. Harris compressed her lips and sat down at her own plate. "I did some research online yesterday."

"What kind of research?"

"Just general. I googled Jeff. I found stories about him as an athlete in that small private high school he went to. Then I found him mentioned in a story while he was in college, at Georgia Tech. Look here." She turned and pulled a sheet of paper off the kitchen counter. She'd printed out a photo and article from the student paper, the *Technique*. "This was from a story about drug dealing in a student dorm there four years ago. I'm sure that's Jeff in the background of the picture."

Sandy took the paper and frowned over it. The story was about two Tech students who'd been arrested and expelled for selling marijuana products and prescription drugs on campus. Two young men in the picture, handcuffed, stood with police officers by a police car. In the background, slightly blurry, was another young man with broad shoulders and dark hair who indeed looked like Jeff.

"It may be," said Sandy. "For heaven's sake, Mom, why were you doing research on Jeff?"

"I've been pretty accurate in predicting students' lives. When he was in my class, I was sure he would get in serious trouble with the law someday. I wanted to know if he had."

Sandy felt a shiver run down her spine. "Has he?"

"He's mentioned down at the end of the story,"

said her mother, pointing. "He's identified as 'Jeffrey Hudson, eighteen, a freshman and roommate of one of the students arrested.' They brought him in for questioning but could find no evidence against him."

Sandy was shocked more at what her mother had done than at what she had found. "Well, *he* wasn't arrested for dealing drugs. You can't help what your roommate does."

"I know, honey. I just wanted to show you this article. Let's see, he was two years ahead of you in school and you've just finished your second year. He must have left Tech the year after this picture was taken, when he was a sophomore. Isn't that strange?"

"I know he's been working on his uncle's farm in North Carolina and came back to Georgia to get a degree in the College of Agriculture and Environmental Sciences."

"Why did he drop out of Tech?"

"I don't know. We haven't had much chance to talk about things like that." Sandy stood up. "We'd better get dressed for church."

Throughout the church service, Sandy thought of how worried her mother must be to do that research. If she herself was a little afraid of her feelings for Jeff, it was not because of her mother's suspicions—it was because of personal doubts when she felt so attracted to him. Was Jeff really interested in her? Perhaps she was just someone he could take on a picnic to help with Bobby. No matter what he said, he might have a relationship with that dark-haired girl.

After the service, her mother's good friend, Peg Morrison—Bill's mother—approached them on the sidewalk outside. "How about going to the Athens Inn for brunch?" she suggested. "Bill and Todd are off at that golf tournament. It would be fun for us girls to get together."

"That would be fun," said Mrs. Harris. "Don't you think so, Sandy?"

"Oh, yes," agreed Sandy, though she really wished she could just go home and start reading for her literature class. She wished it even more during lunch as the two women talked about Bill—how well he had done at school, how well he now spoke Spanish, how good he was with customers at the store, how wonderful that he was back in Athens and seeing Sandy again. It was true, Bill would be the ideal match for her.

That afternoon, Sandy read *Pride and Prejudice*, the next novel for her class, trying not to think of Jeff or Bill as she took notes and tapped in answers to the online class discussion. About midafternoon she heard her phone buzz. It was her friend Kathy.

"Hi. How's the babysitting going?"

"This first week has been great. How is Lake Burton?"

"Oh, it's nice, but I miss Athens already. We just came back for the weekend. Can you come to Ruggeri's tonight?"

Ruggeri's was the Italian restaurant and music venue where many of the town's college students hung out—those attending the University of Georgia and former Athens high school students back for the summer. While on other evenings local bands often performed at Ruggeri's, on Sundays, a retro jukebox provided the only music. The young people who came could insert coins into the slot and dance to vintage songs in the small dance area. But often they just ate pizza, drank beer or soda, and talked. Sandy enjoyed Sunday nights there.

She deliberated only a moment. "Ruggeri's would be fun."

"Great. I'll pick you up about a quarter to six."

"Okay. I'll be on the porch." Sandy tapped the disconnect button. That took care of the rest of her day. She turned her phone to "Do Not Disturb."

****

That Sunday morning, Jeff found himself thinking of Sandy, of being with her and Bobby on the river. Now he wanted to see her again—just her.

He remembered how Mrs. Harris had greeted him coldly the morning before and had said almost nothing when he'd dropped Sandy off that night. Back in fifth grade, she'd preferred students like Bill Morrison, that scrawny blond kid in the class, a teacher's pet who often stayed after school not as a punishment but because he wanted to help her clean up. That kid had been like an irritating insect buzzing at him—calling him names, shooting spitballs at him when Mrs. Harris wasn't looking, writing bad words with chalk on his locker that appeared as if he'd written them. Bill also would avidly watch his fights on the playground, then when they were almost over, run to the teachers to tell. But if he'd wanted to get Jeff's attention with this behavior, he must have been frustrated because Jeff ignored him.

Opening a textbook, he began to read. The material turned out to be interesting, about environmental law. This would relate to his work on the farm. At midafternoon he had a late lunch, then drove to the student gym where he thought he might work out. But there, he ran into some guys from one of his classes, and they invited him to join a pickup basketball game. The physicality of it felt good. His life at Tech now seemed longer ago and farther away than ever. Except for the proximity of his father, perhaps Athens would not be so bad after all.

On the way home, he bought a hamburger at a fast-food place to take back to the apartment, and as he ate it realized he could not call Sandy. He did not know her cell phone number. *Damn.* He could ask his father, but he preferred not to. He dressed in jeans and a clean Oxford shirt, picked up his phone, wallet, and keys, and headed to his car. He would drive to her house. To see her, he thought with a wry grin, he would have to face her gorgon of a mother, like a hero in a Greek myth. But as he pulled up to the curb and stopped, he saw only the next-door neighbor, out in his front yard trimming shrubbery.

The man looked over at him and waved, then walked to the car. "Hi there, son. Can I help you with something?"

"I was just stopping at the Harris's to see…"

"Ah, you must be looking for Sandy. I saw you pick her up yesterday morning. She left with a friend a little while ago. They've probably gone to Ruggeri's—do you know that pizza and beer place? It's downtown on the corner of Broad and Spring Streets."

The "friend" mustn't be male, or he wouldn't have given me directions, thought Jeff. "Thank you, sir. I'll go check for her there." He pulled away from the curb. Looked like he was getting to know Athens again in a pretty short time.

****

As Sandy and Kathy entered Ruggeri's, they saw their sorority sisters, Carole Connolly and Diane Miller, and two other girlfriends, waiting for them. They greeted each other with hugs and laughter, commandeered the big booth, and ordered their usual pizza and sodas. As they chattered enthusiastically about their summer jobs and what they had heard from other friends, Sandy pulled out her phone and took a short video of them.

"Oh, our official photographer! Will you put that on Facebook?" asked Kathy.

"I think I will," said Sandy, as they all clustered around looking at the images. "You all look so good."

She had just posted it when she heard cheery male voices: "Well, look who's here!" Sandy raised her eyes from her phone to see two more Athens childhood friends and UGA classmates—Will Thompson and Tom Dudley—coming through Ruggeri's door. And following them was Bill. Sandy put her phone away quickly. She'd come here with Kathy, when...hadn't Bill said something about seeing her Sunday night?

The three boys came over to the booth. Will and Tom sat down with the girls. "Hey, they haven't finished their pizza," said Tom, reaching toward the platter.

"No, you can't have any," Diane said. "We're going to finish it."

"Aw, I'm hungry," said Tom.

"Cool it," said Bill, standing by the booth. "I'm going to order another—and a pitcher of beer."

The group cheered. Bill walked over to the counter and put in his order, then strolled over to the antique jukebox and inserted a quarter. A 1950s recording with a fast, pulsating beat started playing. "Come on, Miss Harris," said Bill, returning to the booth. "Let's work off some of the calories you've consumed."

Sandy laughed and slid out of the booth, while Will held out his hand to Kathy. Sandy found herself happy to be dancing the old-fashioned jitterbug among her friends. Bill was a good dancer—graceful and agile. Once after a high school dance, her mother, one of the chaperones, had compared him to Fred Astaire.

"He'd probably rather be compared to John Travolta," Sandy had replied.

As the record ended, Sandy stood beside Bill for a moment catching her breath—and then looked around. Immediately, she felt she had lost her breath again—for she saw, leaning against the wall, Jeff Hudson. Had he been watching her dance? Their eyes met for only a second, it seemed, and then he turned toward the door. She left Bill's side, pushed through the dancers still milling about, and caught up to him just as he was pushing it open. "Jeff!" she called, catching his arm. "Don't leave."

"You're with someone," he said.

"I'm with a bunch of friends, that's all. Come back and meet them." He slowly turned back and let the door close. She led him to the booth, where Bill, Kathy, and Will had resumed their seats. As they approached, everyone looked up at them, the girls appraising Jeff with obvious interest.

Sandy spoke to the whole group. "This is Jeff Hudson, who's just transferred to the university. Jeff, this is"—she listed the girls' names and then ended with—"I think you know Will Thompson, Tom Dudley, and...Bill Morrison."

Bill stared at Jeff with intensity, almost as if conveying a hidden message. "Do you remember me? I was in the Lumpkin Street School with you when you lived in Athens. We both had Sandy's mother as a teacher in fifth grade."

The booth quieted now as Jeff looked back at Bill. "Yes, I remember you."

Tom spoke up then. "I was in that class too, Jeff."

"So was I," said Will. "Come, sit down with us."

"Yes, have some pizza," said Carol. "We've got some left."

"Hey, you wouldn't let me have any," said Tom.

"I'm just showing hospitality to a newcomer," said Carol. "And Bill's ordered another."

"I've eaten," Jeff replied. "But thanks."

Bill spoke out again. "So your father is the professor Sandy is working for."

"That's right. I'm staying in his garage apartment for now. That's how I met Sandy."

"We thought you'd left Athens for good."

Sandy felt her heart rate speed up. What was this lingering antagonistic relationship she sensed between Bill and Jeff? She remembered Bill had said "good riddance" when they'd talked about him the night she went to the park with him. Would Bill now say something about Jeff's fights or the school break-in?

"Here comes the pizza," she exclaimed, relieved to change the subject. They all turned to see Mrs. Ruggeri coming up with the big platter.

"See, we've got plenty," Will told Jeff. "Help yourself." But Bill, who had paid for the pizza, did not second the offer, and Jeff said again that he wasn't hungry. Mrs. Ruggeri set the platter on the table, then left and returned with beer mugs and the pitcher of beer for the boys. Sandy sat down in the booth and looked up at Jeff, who was still standing.

"Just sit down, honey," Mrs. Ruggeri told Jeff.

He sat down on the edge of the booth opposite Sandy. Kathy pushed a mug toward him and filled it with beer.

After the division of the pizza slices, Kathy said, "I need to go to the ladies' room. Come with me, Sandy."

"Okay." Sandy smiled and shrugged slightly at Jeff. "I'll be right back."

"So, tell me about that *hot guy* and you?" Kathy said as they stood at the mirror applying lip gloss and brushing their hair.

Sandy studied her reflection in the mirror. "I've really just met him. He moved here on Monday, and yesterday we took his little brother—the child I'm babysitting for—on a picnic. That's all."

"Hmm, well, maybe next time you'll be without the little brother."

"I think Jeff already has a girlfriend."

"So, where is she?" asked Kathy as they left the restroom.

As the two girls approached the booth, Jeff stood up, his beer barely touched, and put his arm around Sandy. "I'm going to take Sandy home now," he said to the group. "She has to babysit for my little brother in the morning."

Bill looked up, his mouth opening in disbelief.

Kathy smiled. "Sure," she said. "Protect your interests."

Jeff laughed at that and gave a general wave. "Nice meeting you all."

Although she felt her friends' surprised eyes upon her, Sandy walked with him through Ruggeri's to the door. Outside, however, she felt the need to assert herself in some way. "You never asked if I wanted to leave."

"I didn't hear you protest," Jeff retorted, now obviously in a good mood. He took her to his SUV and opened the passenger side door for her.

"How did you know where I was?"

"I stopped at your house—your neighbor was out in the yard doing some trimming. He told me."

He got in on the driver's side and turned to her in the dusky interior. "Come here," he said. "I didn't get to do this last night."

She moved closer, leaned over the console, and their lips met. Perhaps he meant it to be just a friendly kiss. But her lips opened and so did his. It was different from kissing John, although that had been sweet and pleasurable. And it was certainly different from Bill's kiss after the movie. This—this kiss, as it continued, was like pushing off into a strong current and losing control of the direction.

When they finally moved apart, both had become breathless. "I didn't expect to find anyone like you here," he said.

She found it hard to focus. "What do you mean?"

"I don't know." He thought a minute. "I guess," he said, "I never thought I'd find anything or anyone here in Athens to like. But I had to come back to Georgia if I wanted to go to the university ag program. And I figured it was time to face the past."

"You mean like those fights on the playground?"

"They were part of it." He paused, as if considering

whether to go on. Then he did. "During that fifth-grade year especially, my father was gone most of the time, working nights in his office, going off on weekends, he said on research trips. When he was home, he and my mother fought constantly. And my mother—she'd started drinking."

Sandy came to complete attention. Jeff turned away from her and stared out of the windshield. "I think…" he finally said, "I now think I really was trying to get into trouble then to make my parents mad at me instead of at each other. And maybe to make them pay attention to me. Then one Saturday night, when my father was gone as usual—and my mom had drunk herself to sleep, I did a really bad thing."

"What?" she asked, though she thought she knew.

"I sneaked out of the house and walked to my school. I guess I was sort of fantasizing about being a criminal, a robber like on some television show. That would be something to shock my parents. Anyway, I got there and broke a window with a rock, knocked out the glass—getting a little bloody in the process…"

Jeff flexed his right hand as if feeling blood on it again. "I climbed inside through the window and went down the hall. It was eerie, so dark and quiet and empty, with just the emergency exit lights on. I got to the principal's office. For some reason, it wasn't locked. I went in and turned on the lights and started going through the drawers of his secretary's desk. I found some money in a box in one drawer. I stuffed it in my pocket and headed back out, back down the hall, to the window. But maybe there'd been some kind of silent alarm when I broke the window. Anyway, two police officers cruising the area saw the office lights and stopped to investigate. When I jumped out of the window, I landed right beside them."

"Oh, no! What did you do?"

Jeff laughed wryly. "What could I do?"

He laid his arm across the back of the seat and gently massaged her shoulder. She reached up and took his hand, looking at it in the dim light, turning it over. She could see white scars crisscrossing the palm. He went on, "They took me to the police station and called my mother. But that's what did it, what broke the family pattern. After that, my mother filed for divorce. The judge gave her and her parents custody. We went to Atlanta to live with them. My grandparents paid a lot of attention to me—and to her. She and I had to have some sessions with a psychologist. I went to a new school. Things got better."

"You didn't see your father after the move?"

The hand, back on her shoulder, was still. For a long moment, he did not answer. "No," he said finally. "The court said I had to spend one weekend a month with him until I was eighteen. I skipped some weekends, but when I did visit him, I'd take the shuttle to Athens and he'd meet me with his current girlfriend. There was a series of them. I guess they'd try and show me a good time, but it made me feel sick if they'd hug and kiss. Sometimes they'd even spend the night in my parents' bed. It was like my father was doing everything he'd been doing that had driven my mother so crazy—but it was out in the open now. Almost as if he was proud of it."

His tone hardened. "I hated those visits. After I turned eighteen and graduated from high school, I went to Georgia Tech. I told him I was never coming back to

Athens. I didn't, not even when he married Glenda. Not until now. That's why I had never seen Bobby."

"But you and he have kept in touch since then?"

"Sort of. We had a kind of truce. When I stopped coming to Athens, he came over to Atlanta sometimes to visit me, just by himself. He'd sent support money to my mother for me through high school, and when I went to Tech, he paid my tuition. He stopped sending any money when I dropped out and went to live with my uncle."

"And now he's letting you stay in his apartment."

Jeff shifted uneasily. "Yes. I should find a place of my own as soon as I can." He removed his hand from her shoulder and turned the key in the ignition.

Sandy watched the dark shapes of trees go by as Jeff drove down the city streets. "I'm sorry you haven't come to feel better about your father now. I think he wants to be your friend. And this must be a hard time for him, left alone with a little boy—"

His voice was again hard. "I'm not sorry for him after what he put my mother through." Then, after a moment he reached over and touched her hand. "Sorry. I shouldn't have unloaded all that about my childhood on you. It's over. I've never talked about it like that to anyone, even the psychologist."

"I'm glad you talked to me." Sandy wondered where he was taking her but did not really care. She kept thinking of how hurt he had been—and still was. On the canoe trip, he had been a strong, protective figure, but now she saw in him that dark-haired young boy being scolded by her mother, in trouble, she now knew, because his family was in crisis. She wanted to hold that young boy and comfort him.

Maybe that was why—or partly why—when Jeff followed a country road up a hill to a field overlooking the lights of town, parked, and turned to her, she dismissed the shadows of doubt of that morning. Putting her arms around his neck, she responded fully to his kisses.

Chapter Six

Jeff hadn't meant for it to happen. First, he'd expected the kiss there in the car outside of Ruggeri's to be just brief and affectionate. Then, as he smelled the clean, flowered scent of her skin, felt her soft hair against his cheeks and her lips opening to his, it became a different kind of kiss. Was that why he had poured out the whole stupid story of his childhood to her? And why he took her to a hill outside of town that he remembered vaguely from years ago on rides with his mother? It was still there, not built up as so many vacant places in Athens now were. He hoped then only that they would kiss again the way they had at Ruggeri's. But when they had, the console between the seats pressed against them, keeping them apart, until they moved to lie in the back of the Durango. There, with that hard barrier gone, and then the softer barriers of their clothing, they came together.

He'd had sex with girls since Sheila, in high school and at Tech—he even carried an almost forgotten condom in his wallet. But with Sandy that night, the sex was different. Yes, it was amazing. But it also was more than physical gratification. She'd shown him not only passion, but a tenderness that satisfied another need within him, one he didn't even realize he had.

As he drove her home afterward, they were silent,

but the silence was beautiful, and her hand on his said it all. "Good night," he said quietly, as he pulled up to the curb in front of her house, and he kissed her forehead as a father or brother might.

She put her hands behind his head, pulled his face down, and pressed her lips again to his. Then, almost as if embarrassed, she opened the car door, jumped out, and ran up the walk to her house, as fleet as the doe they had seen running from the river into the safety of the woods. And he knew he could hardly wait until he saw her again.

****

Oh my God, Sandy thought Monday morning when she woke up, *it really happened—there in the back of Jeff's SUV.* She'd wondered if her next time might be with Bill. But last night with Jeff had not involved experimentation or rational thought, just that sense of being caught in a strong current and then—then a spectacular plunge over white water rapids, unlike anything she'd ever experienced. She burrowed under the sheet and closed her eyes against the light.

Her phone, on the table next to her bed, buzzed. Sitting up to look, she saw Kathy's name on the screen. She had to answer.

"Hi," came the familiar, cheery voice. "I just had to call you before you went to babysit and we left to go back to the lake. I wanted to know what happened last night after you left with Jeff."

"Just a minute." Sandy pushed back her hair and tried to gather her thoughts.

"Are you still asleep? I figured you'd be up if you have to be at work by nine. I bet you were out late last night! And no little brother! Did you have fun?"

Sandy didn't want to share what had happened even with her best friend. "We weren't out very late."

"Bill was pretty upset after you left with Jeff."

"He was?"

"He, Will, and Tom told some stories about Jeff and all his fights in fifth grade. Will and Tom's were partly humorous, but Bill was totally serious. He doesn't trust Jeff even now. I could tell he was getting more and more concerned about you being with him last night."

"Really?"

"But we girls thought Jeff seemed nice—and he's so good-looking! You know, maybe Bill was just jealous. He never liked girls that much in high school, but you and he were always friends, and I think now he wants to get seriously involved with you... I'm glad everything is okay. I've got to go. My parents are ready to leave for the lake. I wish you didn't have this job. I'd love to have you visit us."

"I'd love to, too," Sandy said. "Maybe we can work something out."

She disconnected and lay back in bed. What did Bill think—that Jeff might rape her last night? If so, his worry related to what happened—but it certainly hadn't been rape. Sandy's cheeks flamed.

Her thoughts then turned to her mother. Surely she would never suspect what happened last night. *She doesn't even know I was with Jeff.*

At breakfast, however, something must have shown on her face. Her mother said, "You seem to be kind of glowing today, as if you had a secret. What did you do last night?"

"I was at Ruggeri's with the girls."

"Was Bill there?"

Sandy nodded.

"Last night, I was out on the porch picking up the magazine I'd been reading out there when Mr. Franklin next door saw me. He said a young man with dark hair came by looking for you. That must have been Jeff."

Sandy was silent.

"Did he find you?"

Sandy avoided her mother's eyes. "Yes."

****

After breakfast, Sandy drove to Dr. Hudson's to begin her second week of babysitting. Her eyes went at once to the space where Jeff usually parked, but it was empty. She straightened up the house, then set up the sprinkler for Bobby to play in. At lunchtime, after dressing Bobby in dry clothes, she was fixing whole wheat macaroni and cheese when a tap came on the kitchen door. Before she could answer, it opened. There stood Jeff.

"Hi, lady," he said. His presence and his voice made her feel warm and tingly all over.

"Jeff!" cried out Bobby, running over and hugging his knees.

"Is Sandy fixing you lunch?" Jeff asked, scooping him up.

"Macaroni and cheese!" said Bobby.

"Do you have enough for me too?" Jeff asked her.

"I do." Looking over at him, she wondered if she made him feel as she felt. But they were in the daylight world now, not alone in the dark. So, as Bobby chattered happily about playing in the "vrinkler," the three of them sat around the kitchen table to eat. They had just finished when they heard a car coming in the driveway. Sandy stood up and looked out. "It's your father," she said to Jeff. "He never comes home for lunch. I wonder if something's wrong."

Dr. Hudson hurried up to the kitchen door. Sandy opened it for him. "Well, hello," he said, looking in. "I didn't expect to find such a group here."

"You didn't expect me, you mean," Jeff said. He began to get up as if to leave, but his father said, "Stay here, no problem. I'm glad to see you. I just somehow forgot my phone when I left this morning, and I came back for it."

"There's some macaroni and cheese left," said Sandy, a little nervous, eager to please, and wishing Jeff would be nicer to his father. "Would you like some?"

"No, thanks. I've eaten at the Georgia Center."

"A glass of iced tea then?"

"No—I have to get back. I'll just get my phone." He left the kitchen quickly, and as quickly returned, phone in hand.

"Is there anything from Mommy on your phone?" Bobby piped up.

"There sure is." He tapped the screen and found what he wanted. "She sent us a picture. See?" He held the phone out to Bobby.

The little boy peered at it. "What's she doing?"

Sandy could not hide her interest, and after a moment, Dr. Hudson passed the phone on to her. She saw the attractive young woman with the large horn-rimmed glasses standing with several other young people—all in work clothes—against a rock wall. "They've uncovered an odium, a place where the Romans gave plays and sang odes," said Dr. Hudson. "The Roman civilization spread all around the

85

Mediterranean, and more and more of their buildings and artifacts are being excavated. That's the wall of the odium in the background."

Jeff came over and looked at the phone Sandy was holding.

"She's getting plenty of material for her dissertation," Dr. Hudson went on. "I knew this dig would be good for her."

"When will she come home?" asked Bobby.

"When did I tell you?"

Bobby thought. "Six weeks."

"Five now." Dr. Hudson held up one hand, fingers spread as the child counted them. Then, looking at Sandy, he said, "I have to keep reassuring Glenda that everything is fine here, that I have someone good to take care of Bobby. I think she's glad to hear that he misses her, though." His hand now free, he patted the child's head. "She says she misses you too. We'll Skype with her tonight and you can talk to her." Now he regarded his older son. "Glenda hasn't met you, and she'd like to. Why don't you come?"

"Not tonight," Jeff replied. Perhaps he saw his father's look of disappointment. "Some other time."

Encouraged, Dr. Hudson seemed to think a moment. Then he said, "Well, I have another proposal for you. The anthropology department is having its summer-semester picnic at Memorial Park next Saturday afternoon. I'm taking Bobby—and I wondered whether you'd like to come too. There will be students your age there. And I'd like some of my colleagues and students to meet you.'

"You would?" Jeff paused, then said, "Thanks, but I have plans for Saturday."

"I'm sorry to hear that." Dr. Hudson put his phone in his pocket. "Well, if your plans change, let me know. I've got to go." He tousled the little boy's hair and went out the door. They heard his car start, and Bobby ran to the screen porch to watch him back out of the driveway.

"I wish you had agreed to at least one of his invitations," Sandy said softly. She stacked the plates and took them to the sink. Jeff came over behind her. He put his arms around her waist and nuzzled her cheek. She turned her face to his and their lips met. Hearing Bobby's footsteps as he ran in from the screen porch, they broke apart.

"I have to get back to school too," Jeff said. "Are you going to the pool this afternoon?"

"I'd planned to."

"Swim with us," Bobby begged.

Jeff looked down at him. "For a little while." He turned to Sandy. "I'll meet you there—about two?"

"That would be great."

That afternoon, he joined them at the pool, played with Bobby, then joined Sandy on the pool's edge. But this time, unknown to either of them, a girl with dark hair watched from the other end of the pool.

****

As Jeff and Sandy sat side by side on their towels watching Bobby play in the children's pool, Jeff asked, "Would you like to hear my plans for this weekend?"

"I wondered," said Sandy.

"Actually, I've just made them. Since my father and Bobby will be away in the afternoon, I want you to come over to the apartment, and I'll grill us steaks. We'll have our own picnic."

"It's hard to refuse that offer."

"Good, that's settled." Jeff brushed her cheek with his knuckles. "I think maybe it's time you gave me your cell phone number, don't you?"

She laughed and dictated her number to him. He texted her right then; now she would have his number too. "I'll call you about the time for the picnic," he said. "I'm thinking around three o'clock."

"Okay."

He gathered his things and went to the edge of the kiddie pool to say goodbye to Bobby, who was playing with the two little brothers again. Then, his towel around his neck, he turned, waved to Sandy, and walked away. Sandy watched him go. Smiling a little, she lay back on her towel and, listening to her little charge chatter with his friends, closed her eyes.

Suddenly something came between her and the light and heat of the sun. Opening her eyes, she saw, with a start, someone standing over her. Sandy sat up and, shading her eyes against the glare, saw it was the dark-haired girl she had seen with Jeff at the movie.

"Hi," said the girl. "I'm Sheila Odashion. You're Sandy Harris, right? Can I talk to you for a minute?"

"Sure," Sandy said, though she had a sense of foreboding. How did this girl even know her name?

She sat down beside Sandy. Her hair was long and glossy, her eyes brown, and yes, that slight hook to her nose gave her an exotic look, mature and worldly. "We have a friend in common."

"You mean Jeff."

"Yes, Jeff Hudson. I thought maybe I should give you some background on him. We girls need to stick together sometimes."

We do? You and I? "What do you mean?"

"You know, some guys can really turn on the charm, get what they want from you, then that's it, it's over, they're off with someone else. Guys like Jeff, as the saying goes, sow their wild oats." She laughed. "I suppose some of them grow out of that stage. But my point is, that's the stage Jeff is in right now—in fact, has been for a while. I've known him for years. We were in middle and high school together. I thought, since you've just met him, and since he's clearly turning on to you, that you should know."

"I saw *you* with him at the movies last Friday."

"Yes, we saw you too. Jeff told me who you were. So I guess you know he and I are going out again. But he and I understand each other. I know Jeff is a player. I've seen him with a lot of girls, and I've seen him hurt a lot of girls." She paused. "Your relationship with him is none of my business, but seeing you here, I thought I should warn you about him. Jeff is fun, I'll admit. So have fun with him. But don't think you're the only one." She stood up. "There, I've told you. I'm sorry, but I felt I had to."

Sandy bristled at her intrusion, at her supposedly worldly-wise and experienced advice. "I appreciate your concern," she said. "But I can handle this myself. It was nice meeting you."

"Nice meeting you. See you." Sheila walked back to the other end of the pool slowly, a bit sensuously.

I won't believe her, Sandy thought. *She's just jealous. I remember how she cuddled up to Jeff at that movie. She saw me with him here at the pool.*

Yet, she couldn't help it; the girl had reactivated those personal shadows of doubt. She said she'd known him for years. They were "going out again."

But could there be some truth to what she'd said about him being a player?

****

Two days later, his classes and a stint at the library over, Jeff threw his books in the back seat of the Durango and headed to the garage apartment. As he was driving down East Campus Road, his phone music played. He glanced at its screen, visible on the seat beside him. It was his uncle. Without a Bluetooth in his old SUV, he pulled off to the shoulder to answer.

"Uncle Jake," he said, "is everything all right?"

"I'm in Athens," came his uncle's voice. "I drove down to Atlanta to see your mother, and thought I'd stop and see you on the way back."

"I'm surprised you left the farm."

"I figured I could take a couple days off. The crew can take care of things. I miss you up there, though."

"I can meet you back at the apartment. Do you know my father's address?"

"Sure I know it. I'm there now."

"I'm only a few minutes away." Jeff clicked off the connection. He felt a nagging worry. Why had his uncle come to Atlanta, then here? He wondered if something was wrong with his mother.

When he turned into the driveway, he saw his uncle's truck parked in front of the stairway to the apartment, "Rushing Creek" painted on the doors, with a picture of a fast-flowing mountain stream. He walked over to it, feeling a surge of homesickness for the farm. Uncle Jake, sitting in the front seat, got out and wrapped him in a hug. "Hello there, boy."

"Hey, Uncle Jake." Jeff extricated himself from his uncle's wiry arms. "Come on up." He led his uncle up the long set of steps at the side of the garage, unlocked the apartment, and motioned him in. "I'll get the AC on. Sit down."

Uncle Jake sat at the kitchen table, looking around at the unmade sofa bed, the papers and books scattered on the coffee table, the breakfast dishes in the sink.

"Sorry about the mess," said Jeff. "I had an early class. Would you like a drink? A Coke? A beer?"

"Just a glass of water."

Jeff placed one in front of him, poured himself one, and sat at the table with him. "You've been to see my mother?"

His uncle rotated the water glass in his large hands. "Yes, I figured I'd better check on her."

"She's not drinking again, is she?"

"She said she wasn't. And Mom and Dad said they hadn't seen her drinking, that she still went to her AA meetings. It wouldn't hurt for you to go over and see her when you can. You're only an hour or so away."

His mother worked at a cosmetics counter in an Atlanta department store. "Did she say anything about her job?"

"No. She's still working several days a week…But I think she was upset about you living here in your father's apartment."

"You arranged that."

"But I didn't realize it would bother her after all these years."

Jeff shifted in his chair. It had, after all, bothered him too. "I'll go see her soon. We talk on the phone. We text and email a lot. Same as always."

"That's good. Look, I can't stay, I have to get back to the farm tonight. I just wanted to see the apartment, talk to you about your mom. See if you were doing all right."

"I miss the farm, but actually, I like it here. I'm glad you made me come."

His uncle paused a moment, then asked, "No contacts from the past?"

Jeff shot his uncle a glance. "No. Well, just an old girlfriend from high school. Nothing else."

"That's good." His uncle stood and clapped him on the back. "I need to get on the road."

"We could go out and grab a bite to eat."

"If it's quick."

As the two went back down the stairs, Dr. Hudson pulled into the driveway and parked beside the truck. "Ah, hello, Jake," he called out, opening the car door. He strode over and the two men shook hands. "Good to see you. What brings you here?"

"I just visited Sibyl and thought I'd stop by and see Jeff on the way back to North Carolina. That's a great apartment you've provided for him—though he's not the best housekeeper."

"Well, he's busy," replied his father. "I'm glad to have him here. How is Sibyl?"

"She's fine."

Jeff looked at his father, then Uncle Jake. The two men were certainly friendly to each other, and that surprised him. It would seem his mother's older brother would resent the man who had cheated on his sister and made her so unhappy she started drinking.

A door slammed at the back of the house and Bobby burst out, Sandy following. "Daddy!" the little boy called, running to Dr. Hudson.

His father picked him up, put him on his shoulders,

and turned to Jake. "This is my son Bobby. And this is Sandy Harris. Glenda is on a dig for a few weeks this summer, and while I'm working, Sandy takes care of Bobby. She and I are sort of a tag team."

"Sandy, this is Jake Thompkins—my Uncle Jake," Jeff said.

She held out her hand. "I'm glad to meet you. Jeff told me he'd been working on your farm the last couple of years."

"Best worker I ever had," he said, taking Sandy's hand and regarding her with interest.

"He's the one who talked me into coming here to school," said Jeff.

Bobby looked down at Uncle Jake from his perch on his father's shoulder. "Jeff teaches me to swim at the pool."

"Does he? I bet he's a good teacher."

"Jake and I are going to grab a sandwich, and then he has to head back," said Jeff. He looked at Sandy. "I'll call you later."

****

"The Morrisons have invited us for a barbecue at their house Saturday afternoon," Sandy's mother told her when she got home that day. "We hope you and Bill will eat with us older folks before you two go off somewhere."

"Bill and I aren't doing anything together Saturday," said Sandy. She drew in a breath. She couldn't put off telling her mother any longer. "I'm going to be with Jeff."

"You what?" exclaimed Mrs. Harris. "You said you weren't going to see him after that canoe trip."

"I like him, Mom. I want to see him again."

"Peg and I assumed you and Bill would be doing something together on Saturday. He seemed to think so." Mrs. Harris came over to Sandy and put her hands on Sandy's shoulders. "Honey, I know I can't tell you what to do or not do...but I really don't like you seeing Jeff. I've seen too many problem children grow up to be problem adults. And I'll bet he *was* involved with those drug dealers at Georgia Tech..."

"I don't think so." Sandy broke away. "I'll set the table for dinner." She did not need these comments about Jeff right now: Bill's reported concern about her, Sheila's warning Monday at the pool—and now her mother's suspicions again. With a clatter of plates and silverware, Sandy vented her frustration while avoiding further discussion.

Lying on her bed after dinner, Sandy continued reading *Pride and Prejudice*. She'd read it in high school and knew the plot. Elizabeth Bennett starts out prejudiced against the rich, aristocratic Darcy, whom she considered proud and impolite. She feels attracted to Wickham, an army officer who, in contrast, seems warm and charming. But later, Elizabeth finds out Wickham is really a deceptive rake and Darcy the worthy, generous hero. The two men are the opposite of what she'd thought them to be, and the first-time reader is probably deceived along with her.

Sandy's phone buzzed. Jeff? She looked at the screen. It was Bill. She swiped the answer slider.

"Hey, Sandy." Bill sounded accusing. "What's going on with you?"

"What do you mean?"

"You and Jeff Hudson."

"I don't know what's going on," she said.

"You and he looked like you did at Ruggeri's Sunday night. I've been thinking about that ever since. I was so upset I waited to call you. And now my mother says you won't come to our barbecue Saturday. That you're doing something with him."

"You and I are free to go out with other people."

"I thought our relationship was changing, that we'd be dating. You've blindsided me. And *Jeff Hudson*?"

Sandy said nothing.

"We need to talk. Can I come over tonight?"

"I have to get some reading done for my class tomorrow."

"Tomorrow night, then."

"Bill, with this job and my class I'm really busy this week."

"All right, but you're making a real mistake if you get involved with Jeff." Before he hung up, there was an ominous tone in his voice, as if he knew something she didn't.

That night in bed, Sandy lay awake. Her mother's suspicions that Jeff at Tech had been linked to sales of illegal drugs were totally unfounded. The article her mother had shown her didn't show him guilty of anything. But what was behind Bill's strange warnings?

She tossed to the other side of the bed. Waiting there were thoughts of what the girl at the pool had said—her descriptions of Jeff's many relationships with girls. That night they'd made love, he had been prepared with a condom, had been so efficient with it that it hadn't interrupted the mood at all. Didn't that show that he was sexually experienced, the kind of player Sheila said he was?

She then thought of the advice her mother had

given her about sex. "*Wait until you really know and trust a boy before you get sexually involved. That takes time.*" Her great-grandmother's advice, those last days in the nursing home, had been even stricter. "*Never, ever sleep with a boy until you and he are married.*"

What had happened with Jeff Sunday night in his SUV had been so exhilarating, felt so right. He seemed to be feeling the wonder of it just as she did. After Jeff had told her about his childhood, she'd felt that he had shared something special and private with her, that she did "really know" him.

But it was true, she'd fallen for Jeff as quickly as Aunt Mary had fallen for her first husband. And she didn't know why he'd left Tech. Maybe, after all, things *were* happening too fast between her and Jeff. Saturday on the picnic at his apartment, she'd try to determine if she should put brakes on this relationship.

Chapter Seven

On Friday evening, Sandy and her mother were eating supper in the kitchen when a knock came on the back door. "Hello, Bill," Mrs. Harris exclaimed after opening the door. "This is a surprise! Can you sit down and have some supper with us?"

"That would be great," said Bill, stepping into the kitchen. "I've come directly from work."

Sandy's mother bustled about, fixing him a plate of rice, grilled chicken, and steamed asparagus while he took a seat. He looked over at Sandy a little tentatively. She lowered her eyes.

"How is work going?" Mrs. Harris asked, putting the food before him and sitting down with them.

"It's fine. Dad's giving me more responsibilities. He wants me to work with him in the store once I get this MBA."

"That'd be wonderful. Do you think you will?"

"I think so. Maybe it's time I moved back home." He looked at Sandy, and she made herself smile. "The city has been doing some work at Memorial Park," he said. "Their landscape guys bought some of the plants and supplies from our store. I thought maybe you'd like to go over there and see the new gardens, take some pictures. Maybe we could use them in ads for the store. My dad told me about the prizes you've won."

"Oh, I don't—" Sandy began.

"That's a good idea," interrupted her mother. "Sandy loves gardens, don't you, dear?"

In spite of herself, Sandy began to feel the old excitement about taking photos. She had dreamed, when dating John, of becoming a photojournalist. "All right, then, for a little while."

After supper, Mrs. Harris told them not to worry about the dishes, but to go on to the park while it was still "the golden hour" before sunset, the best time for taking photos. Sandy picked up her purse, her tripod, and her DSLR and went out with Bill to his car. She dreaded what he would say to her, but he just talked about how busy the store had been and asked about her babysitting. At the park, he walked with her along the new garden beds, pointing out different plants as she took several pictures.

It was not until they were on the way home in the dark that he began the conversation she been afraid was coming. "So," he said, looking over at her, "you had a good time with Jeff Hudson Sunday night?"

Even though she'd started having doubts about her relationship with Jeff, Sandy felt she had to be honest. "Yes, I did."

"He didn't get in any fights—didn't rob any gas stations? Didn't meet up with any drug traffickers?"

"What are you talking about?" she said, appalled at his last comment. "You're just making things up because of how he was in fifth grade."

Bill drove on a little. "Okay, sorry. But I thought you and I had planned to see each other on Sunday. When I called you, your phone was off. So I met Will and Tom and went to Ruggeri's. I figured I'd find you there. I thought we were going to start dating. I didn't expect you to leave with Hudson."

"I didn't think you and I had an official date," she replied. "And we never agreed to date exclusively. I want you to feel free to ask out other girls, and I hope you don't mind if I go out with other guys. That's how it was in high school."

"The guys I saw you dating in high school were good guys, and I knew you weren't really involved with them. But Jeff—well, he's different." He paused. "Girls are impressed by those jock types."

"He's not a *jock type*!"

"He looks that way. Look, I worry about you with him. It's just a gut feeling I have. I want you to know."

"You're being honest with me. I'll be honest with you. I don't know yet exactly what's happening between Jeff and me, but I like him, and yes...I *am* seeing him tomorrow. That's why I can't come to the barbecue at your house. You know you and I are still friends."

"Come on, what's with this 'friends' stuff? You and I kissed after the movie."

Sandy remained silent. She did not want to comment on the nature of that kiss.

Bill was pulling up now in front of her house. She got out and gathered her photography equipment from the back seat. "No, I can get this," she said when he moved to help her. "Goodnight, Bill. After I edit my pictures, I'll send them to you."

"Sandy!" he called after her as she went up the walk. She turned back. "We will keep on seeing each other, won't we?"

"Of course. You've been my friend all my life."

"About Jeff then—as a *friend*, I'm telling you. Be careful."

****

Saturday afternoon grew hot and cloudy, but the weather didn't really matter to Sandy as she drove the now-familiar route to the Hudson house for the picnic with Jeff. She knew she looked nice. Her hair, freshly washed, fell shiny over her shoulders, and she wore a flowered, slightly off-the-shoulder blouse with her white ankle pants. As she pulled into the parking area by the garage, Jeff came up to meet her. He opened her car door and put his hand caressingly on the back of her neck. "Hiya, lady."

As Sandy looked at him, the possibility that he had sold drugs at Tech never crossed her mind. But she felt his physical magnetism and remembered what Sheila had said. *Is Jeff a player? Has he been with her since I last saw him?*

"What have you been doing this week?"

He leaned in, kissed her. "Missing you."

A player response.

Jeff turned then and indicated a grill he'd set up near the stairs to his apartment. "I've started the charcoal," he said. "But it will take a while for the coals to be ready. You, lady, will be in charge of the salad. I've got lettuce and a bunch of other things up in the apartment. You've got to do the skilled part—put everything together."

They climbed the stairs and entered the apartment. It was almost chilly inside, cooled by the air conditioner unit throbbing in a window. A sleeper-sofa was opened out into a bed, with Jeff's sleeping bag on it. On a table beside the bed lay a heavy textbook with a title about

100

environment and government regulation. A bar-like counter separated this living-sleeping area from a small kitchen, with an apartment-sized refrigerator, sink, and stove. Everything looked neat and clean.

"What a nice apartment," she said.

"Though I can only stretch really straight in the middle of it," said Jeff, raising his arms and touching the sloping ceiling. His lifted T-shirt revealed his flat, corrugated abdomen. As Sandy laughed, feeling tingles in her own abdomen, he walked over and put his arms around her. "It's good to have you here," he said, and his voice was husky.

She let him hold her against him for a moment, then made herself pull back. "And we don't even have a class assignment to work on."

Jeff let his arms drop and looked at her appraisingly. "Your assignment is the salad."

He led her to the kitchen area and, opening the refrigerator, showed her the lettuce, cucumber, tomato, purple onion. "There. I'll watch." He pulled over a wooden chair and straddled it backward, his arms resting on the back.

Somewhat uneasy under his scrutiny, Sandy took out the ingredients and began tearing the prewashed lettuce into a large bowl he'd set out.

"Why did you say that just now?" he asked after a moment.

"What did I say?"

"Something about having a class assignment to work on."

"Oh, that. Nothing. I've just been thinking, that's all, about the different phases we all go through in life. At this age, it's fun to date different people, to have variety." She reached for a knife and began to slice the onion. Her hand felt slightly shaky.

Jeff stood abruptly and came to her side. He held her wrist so she had to stop slicing. "What is it?"

She wiped her eyes with her other hand. "This onion is getting to me." Then she said, "It's nothing. I just wanted to tell you that I think nothing is wrong with variety. I don't mind if you want that. It's what I want, too."

Jeff let go of her wrist. "You sound like my mother."

"Your mother?"

"She has always said it's bad to date just one person when you're young. She says that was the problem with her and my father. She'd gone to an all-girls boarding school and never dated until she met my father. And he'd gone to a military academy and hadn't known many girls. They met their first year in college, dated only each other—and married right after graduation. She worked to help support him while he got his PhD, and they had me. They hadn't had much experience with the opposite sex except for each other. She thinks that's why, after my father got his job here, he got restless."

"And so you're following your mother's advice? About variety?"

"Maybe I did for a while."

For a while? Is he saying he's ready to settle down? Still, we've barely met. I should never have let myself...

"So how do you know your father was seeing other women while he was still married? Or is that just what your mother told you?"

Jeff seemed to do a double take. "You think she made that up?"

"I don't know. Maybe you should hear your father's side of the story."

"He never gave me his side. He didn't need to. I saw him with a different woman almost every time I visited."

"But that was after the divorce, wasn't it?"

"Well, at any rate, he was getting variety," Jeff said, as if asserting by will his old view. "So, yes, I've dated a lot of different girls over the years. If I ever do get married, I don't want to do what my father did." He looked at her closely. "Have you been talking to someone?"

"I ran into an old friend of yours, that's all."

"Who?" he asked, suddenly on alert. Then he seemed to relax. "Never mind. I think I know. Sandy— let's forget all this!" He pulled her to him and kissed her, and she felt Sunday night's rush of passion. When he drew back, he said, "Let's just enjoy this time together."

"Yes," she replied. It was all she could say.

He took two steaks from the refrigerator, turned, and went out the door. She heard his footsteps as he went down the stairs. She leaned back against the kitchen counter, trying to calm her breathing. Then, over the sound of the air conditioner, she thought she heard her name. She went out to the little landing at the top of the stairs. The hot, heavy air struck her ominously after the cool apartment. He stood at the grill, checking the sizzling meat.

"Did you call?" she asked.

"Yes. Bring my phone when you come down. It's

by the couch."

Sandy took another look at the dark sky, then went inside, found the phone, and went down the stairs.

"I thought we'd better check the weather." He and Sandy sat down at the nearby redwood picnic table, and he looked at his phone screen. "Thunderstorms, possibly heavy at times," he read. "Tornado watch for Clarke and Oconee counties." He looked up at the black, churning clouds. "I hope my father and Bobby have a place to go at that department picnic."

"They have shelters at the park."

"That's something at least. Maybe this will pass over. It doesn't look good, though, does it?"

"I never saw it look exactly like this," she said.

"We'd better eat inside. How do you like your steak?"

"Medium rare."

"Ah, so do I."

She went up to finish the salad, and Jeff brought up the steaks. While the hum of the air conditioner blocked out any sounds from outside, they ate on paper plates and drank beer out of cans.

"And now for dessert," Jeff said.

He led her to the sofa bed. There, as it had that night in the SUV, the world receded.

****

Afterward, lying close together, Jeff said. "Is this just 'fun' for you, Sandy?"

"It's more than that."

"You said you liked variety."

"I just said that because I thought you did." She paused. "I've been with only one other guy before you, someone I dated my freshman year and part of last year at the university. He's gone now…And it wasn't anything like this."

"It wasn't?"

She felt herself blush. "This…with you…is so incredible."

"With us together." Jeff propped himself up on his elbow, leaned over, and kissed her again. But as she pressed closer against him, he drew back. She looked at him, puzzled. "What is it?"

He ran a forefinger over her cheek. "I'd better tell you something. About me."

Sandy's heart jumped. "What?"

A sharp crack of thunder, heard even through the noise of the air conditioner, stopped him. The machine abruptly silenced. The power had gone off. Now they could hear the sound of wind outside.

Jeff sat up. "I'd better go see what's happening." He pulled on his jeans and T-shirt. Sandy reached for her clothes as well. By the time she got out to the landing, rising gales whipped her hair, and the clouds seemed to be writhing in twisted masses. The shrill blast of the tornado warning signal suddenly pierced the air. She had not heard it except during the siren test once a month on the first Wednesday.

"We'd better get to the basement of my father's house," Jeff shouted over the noise. "This garage is not safe. Damn!"

"What?"

"The house is locked. I wouldn't take a key from my father. Well, we can break in."

Dashing back into the apartment, Jeff found a flashlight and snatched his sleeping bag, car keys, and phone, while Sandy picked up her purse. Their phones buzzed simultaneously with a warning alert from the university, but there was no need to hear the message. They rushed down the stairs and toward the house. Debris blew against them—dust, leaves, sharp twigs from trees. Jeff held the sleeping bag around them as a kind of shield. Stopping at the first basement window of the house, he kicked out a pane, reached in through the splintered glass hole, unlocked, and opened the window.

"Climb through," he yelled to Sandy over the howl of the wind.

Sandy squeezed through, Jeff right behind her. Outside, a white sheet of rain began pouring down. Jeff pointed his flashlight into the darkness, and its beam found a laundry table. He dragged it into a corner away from the broken window. They huddled together under the table, Jeff holding Sandy's face against his chest, his hand behind her head. Outside, a noise like a freight train bearing down upon them vibrated the house, and a strong, invisible force sucked at its windows.

And then it became quiet except for the pounding of the rain. Sandy looked up at Jeff. He had raised his head and was listening. "It's passed," he said. "I just hope my father and Bobby…"

"Oh, God, yes," she said, "and my mother."

They came out from under the table and stood. Jeff looked at her, and then his look grew more intense. "Are you hurt?"

"I don't think so." She raised her hand to her cheek. It came away red and wet, but she felt no pain. "It's yours."

He raised his own hand—a deep gash at the base of his thumb was bleeding. He'd gotten the blood on her as he'd held her. "I guess I'm still not very good at breaking windows."

"We'd better bandage that cut. Come on upstairs."

On the first floor, the house seemed unharmed, but it was filled with the gloom and silence that comes when there is no electricity. In the bathroom, Sandy found first aid cream, gauze, and adhesive tape. She rinsed Jeff's wound, put on the cream and a thick padding of gauze, then taped it tightly. "I think you're going to need stitches."

"A lot of people may be hurt worse," he said.

****

When they next looked outside, the rain had stopped, but ambulance and police sirens began to wail.

Jeff turned on his phone and read to Sandy from a local weather site: *"A tornado passed over Athens at approximately five this evening and appears to have touched down on North Milledge Avenue. It has downed trees and wires in many places, and damaged several houses, mostly on Milledge Avenue. Residents are asked to stay in their homes to avoid power lines on the ground. Police are patrolling to give help when needed, and crews are working to clear trees and repair the lines. Parts of North Milledge Avenue will be blocked off until the road is cleared."*

They went to the kitchen and looked out toward the garage. Its roof was gone, many of its shattered pieces lying haphazardly at the back of the lot. In the driveway, a limb was lying across Jeff's Durango. Walking onto the side porch, they saw the screen ripped and the floor covered with debris. At the front of the house, a large pine lay uprooted. By the road, power lines dangled, shooting sparks. Even as they watched, a

Georgia Power truck pulled up.

"I'm going to talk to the crew," said Jeff. "I'll see if they know anything about your neighborhood—and Memorial Park. I'll be right back."

She saw one of the crew members come over to him. She turned from the porch and went to the bathroom. Before busy with Jeff's injury, she now looked at herself in the mirror. She saw her hair bedraggled and damp, her cheek and blouse smeared with blood. She washed her face. Hearing Jeff come back in, she went out, filled with apprehension, to hear what he had learned.

"No tornado touched down at Memorial Park," he told her, "or on your street."

Sandy breathed a deep sigh of relief. They went outside. Jeff pulled the limb from his SUV, exposing a dent but no major damage. He began moving the smaller limbs from the driveway while Sandy, the incipient photojournalist values kicking in, took her phone from her purse and began taking pictures. The crew had just finished clearing the road in front of the house when Dr. Hudson's car turned into the drive.

He jumped out and approached Jeff anxiously. "You're okay?"

"Yes."

"Thank God!"

"How about you?"

"I'm fine."

The two—the middle-aged man, the muscular, younger one—stood there, facing each other. Sandy averted her eyes. It was a private moment between them. It was over quickly, but she felt that the concern they showed for each other in this crisis marked an important change in their relationship.

"Sandy's here," she heard Jeff say.

"I'm okay, too," she told them. "Jeff broke a window to get in your basement, and we waited out the storm there."

"Where is Bobby?" Jeff asked.

"With the weather forecast being so bad, the picnic moved to a faculty member's house, and when the sirens went off, we went to his basement. Afterward, we heard about the tornado touching down in our neighborhood, so I left him there and came right back to see about you. I had to wait by the entrance for a while—they'd blocked off the road."

Jeff pointed to the end of the driveway. "The garage roof is gone."

"Yes—I see. That can be repaired, though. You're what's important."

"Jeff cut his hand," Sandy said. "I think he needs stitches."

Dr. Hudson turned toward his car. "Now that the roads are getting clearer, Jeff, I should be able to get you to the emergency room to check on that. And Sandy, we'll take you home. You'll have to leave your car here until we can get clear these bigger limbs off the driveway."

Jeff and his father sat in the front seat, and Sandy got in the back. They drove slowly up Milledge Avenue, avoiding debris and looking at the destruction about them—trees down, some on top of houses or cars, some roofs partially missing, a small Volkswagen turned on its side. There was the smell of fresh wood in the air. Sandy raised her phone and took pictures out of the car window.

Once they left the Milledge area, the roads were clearer, and as they pulled up to Sandy's house on Catawba Avenue, she saw with relief that it was unharmed. Her mother stood in the yard. Seeing Dr. Hudson's car approach, she ran up to the curb. Sandy jumped out and hugged her. "I'm so glad you're safe," her mother cried. "I heard that the tornado touched down in the Hudson's neighborhood."

"It did, but Jeff was wonderful." Sandy turned to him as he got out of the car and came to her side. "He broke a window because the house was locked and got us in the basement. The garage roof blew off. If we'd stayed in the apartment…"

"I'd better get Jeff to the emergency room to see about that hand," Dr. Hudson called to them, still at the wheel of the Prius.

"Hello, Dr. Hudson," said Mrs. Harris. "Jeff is hurt?"

Jeff held up his hand. "Sandy bandaged me up pretty well."

Sandy's mother nodded. "Of course. She's taken a first aid class."

There was a moment of silence. He and Sandy looked at each other, touched hands. Then he got back in the car, and Dr. Hudson drove away. Sandy turned and, seeing her mother's eyes upon her, straightened her blouse, smoothed her hair.

"Come on, let's go in," Mrs. Harris said. Together, the two walked to the house.

****

"The hospital emergency room will probably be full," said Dr. Hudson. "I think it would be faster to go to student health services for that hand. You have your

110

student ID with you?"

Jeff reached to his pocket and patted his wallet. "I do." He looked sideways at his father. He had seemed truly concerned about him after the tornado. Somehow it was a revelation, yet he didn't know what to make of it. It undermined all he had thought and felt about his father all these years.

Dr. Hudson turned into a circular driveway in front of a low, yellow brick building not far from the student center. The two got out and walked inside. Several students sat in the waiting room, one holding an ice pack to his face, one cradling a hurt arm. Jeff and his father walked up to the check-in desk. "Why, hello, Dr. Hudson," said the plump woman sitting there, smiling in recognition. She had brown hair back in a bun and looked to be in her late thirties.

"Jenny, hello. I didn't know you worked here. This is my son, Jeff. Jeff, this is Jenny—is it Green?"

"Jenny Vickers now. Glad to meet you, Jeff. What can we do for you?"

Jeff spoke. "I cut my hand on a shard of glass. My—my girlfriend thinks it needs stitches."

Jenny looked at his bandaged hand, a little blood seeping through. "I'll need your student ID." She photocopied it, took a few notes. "Dr. Moran will check that out. It shouldn't be too long a wait." She handed him a slip of paper. "How are you, Dr. Hudson?"

"I'm fine." He turned to his son. "Jenny was in one of my anthropology classes a long time ago—how long ago was it, Jenny?"

"Golly, it's been years," she replied. "You'd just come to the university. Jeff, I remember your father mentioning you in class."

"He did?" said Jeff. "It wasn't anything bad, I hope."

"Oh, no. I think you were only about five years old. He talked about how you liked to collect things—arrowheads, other Indian artifacts. He said he hoped you'd go into anthropology too. Did you?"

"No." A vague memory came back to him, like a puff of smoke—of going on an excursion with his father, of finding a smooth, rounded rock in a field that his father said the Creek Indians had used for grinding corn. Funny, he had forgotten that. He turned his attention back to Jenny. "I've just transferred here, to the ag school."

"That's a good school—and that's a good field too," she said. "It's great to see you again, Dr. Hudson. I never forgot your class. You were such a good teacher. I even read one of your books later, the one about family structure of Native Americans in the Southeast. When I was in your class, you told us you were working on that book. I'm so glad I read it. It was fascinating."

Dr. Hudson beamed. "Jenny, you made my day."

"And I'm glad to meet you, Jeff. I hope you like the university."

As another student entered the health center and approached the desk, the two of them went on to the waiting area. Jeff, sitting beside his father, again looked at him. Academic books took a lot of research, black holes of time. Could his father really have been doing research during all those trips he took, really been writing a book all those nights in his office?

Chapter Eight

"The weather looked so bad I considered calling the Morrisons and suggest canceling the barbecue," Sandy's mother said as they entered the house. "Then I heard the tornado siren and went to the basement. I was so worried about you over there at Dr. Hudson's."

"I was worried about you, too."

"Thank heavens we're both all right." Mrs. Harris stepped back and looked at her daughter. "Honey, you look exhausted. You should go upstairs, clean up, and rest awhile."

"Thanks, Mom, I'll do that." *Can she tell what Jeff and I did before the tornado?*

Upstairs, after throwing off her soiled clothes and putting on her bathrobe, Sandy lay on the bed. Then she remembered: Jeff had been about to tell her something. It sounded important. What could it have been? Whatever it was, she knew her feelings for him now. She felt closer to Jeff than she ever had. Realizing that was calming, and she fell into a deep sleep.

When a tentative knock roused her, the room was dark. "Come in," she said.

Her mother opened the door a crack and beamed a flashlight into the room. "Bill is here."

Drowsily Sandy lifted her head. Ripples of irritation rose up in her. Was he here to warn her about

113

Jeff again? Then she remembered the tornado. Had he or his parents been injured, and he'd come to tell them? "Is he all right?"

"He just wanted to check on us—especially you. He knew you were at the Hudson's and that the tornado hit their neighborhood. I told him you were fine, just tired, and had gone to sleep. But he seemed so concerned that I thought I'd tell you he was here. He wants to see you."

"Yes, I should see him." Tying her bathrobe belt tighter around her waist, she went down the stairs behind her mother.

With the electricity still out, the living room was lit by candles. Bill sat in a chair, his long legs out in front of him. He jumped up when she entered. "They say two people on North Milledge were killed when a tree fell on their house. The Hudson's house is near there. I had to see if you were all right."

Sandy was touched by his concern. "I'm fine. When the tornado siren went off, Jeff and I went into the basement of the house. How about you?"

"Everything is all right at home. My dad and I just checked the store. There's some damage but nothing that can't be fixed."

"Would you like something to drink? A gin and tonic?" Mrs. Harris asked. "We still have ice."

"No, thank you," said Bill. "I should let Sandy go back to sleep."

"It was so nice of you to come over," Sandy said as she walked with him to the door and out onto the porch.

"Can I see you tomorrow night?"

Seeing his worried, earnest expression, she nodded. "All right."

It will be a good time, she thought, *to tell him about Jeff and me.*

****

After Jeff and his father left the health center, they picked up Bobby and returned home. Darkness had fallen. "You'll have to stay here in the house tonight—and for a while, until the garage roof is fixed," his father said.

"Sounds good," said Jeff. "Tomorrow I'll see what's left in the apartment."

The two entered the house together, Dr. Hudson carrying Bobby. By the light of a flashlight, he got the little boy into his pajamas, brought him out to say goodnight to Jeff, and then tucked him into bed.

"How about a beer?" Dr. Hudson asked as he came out of Bobby's room. "I think we could both use one."

"Maybe more than one," said Jeff.

Dr. Hudson went to the kitchen and pulled two cans of beer from the refrigerator. Jeff took the offered can from his father, and they sat down in the living room. Dr. Hudson placed the flashlight on the coffee table.

"There's something I need to ask you," Jeff said after a few swallows.

"What's that?"

Jeff hesitated, then spoke quickly. "*Were* you having affairs when you were married to Mom?"

Dr. Hudson laughed ruefully and looked down at the beer between his hands. "Sibyl sure thought so."

"Was she right?"

His father raised the beer can and drank. "No."

"What were you doing all those nights at your office and those weekends you were away?"

115

"You heard Jenny at the health office. I was teaching, doing research, writing a book. The project just kept growing. I had to get that book published to keep my job—to get tenure." He looked over at Jeff. "I admit I was at fault. I should have better explained to Sibyl about what I was and why, tried harder to make her understand, and not been away so much."

"You and she must not have been like that when you were first married, in grad school."

"I didn't have to be gone so much. And when I was, she wasn't so alone. We lived in grad student housing. She had a lot of support from the other students there. She had a part-time job in a women's clothing boutique in Madison and took you to a nursery school for faculty members' children. Everything worked out well then. She was happy, you were happy, I was happy." He drained his beer. "You ready for another?"

"Sure." He watched his father walk into the kitchen and return with a can in each hand. Taking one of them, he said, "I don't understand why things changed so much after you moved here."

"She didn't have the same kind of support. The other faculty wives were older or had jobs of their own. I suggested she check out the clothing stores in Athens for a sales position like the one she had in Madison, but there were no openings. You were in public school most of the day by then, and she was isolated in this house. She wanted to have another baby, but that didn't happen. And I *was* away too much."

"She started to drink."

His father nodded.

"A lot," said Jeff.

116

"By the time I got tenure, she was really drinking and suspicious of me, and I—I got in the habit of staying away. I liked my office. It had become my home. So it's true I was not a good husband. And I was not being a good father to you."

Jeff licked his lips. "That last year she told me she was going to commit suicide."

Dr. Hudson jerked his head up and looked at Jeff. "She said that to me. I never knew she said that to you."

"She told me you were having affairs, maybe were in love with someone else, that you were going to leave us. After the divorce, when I visited you, and you were dating all those different women, I thought that was proof she was right. Why didn't you tell me if it wasn't true? You never said anything."

Dr. Hudson stood up and paced across to the fireplace. "She was absolutely convinced I was involved with other women—especially that last year when I had a female research assistant. She got really crazy on that subject. When I came home, she would ask me about where I went, check my pockets, my briefcase, even my laptop. She got pretty hysterical some nights. I was afraid you would hear us. Only later did Jake and her parents tell me she'd always been fragile psychologically. That's why they sent her away to a safe private girls' high school."

He crunched the second empty beer can in his hand. "I didn't want to tell you about all that. I didn't want to say anything bad to you about your mother, especially because I felt a lot of it was my fault. And after the divorce, she got better. She went to AA, found some work in the department store." He paused. "You were just a kid. I knew she was angry at me, but I thought she was taking good care of you. I didn't know she'd told you those things."

"She did."

"Maybe that was why you...by your fifth-grade year, the school described you as incorrigible. After Sibyl and I decided to divorce, the judge thought it would be better for you to get away from here, live with your mother and her parents. I thought that would be best, too. I knew her parents would be there for you both when I hadn't been."

"But you didn't deny having affairs when the judge made that decision."

His father turned from the fireplace toward Jeff. "I only said I hadn't been a good husband or father. I'm trying to make up for that now with Glenda and Bobby. They are my second chance. But I want Glenda to have her own career and not be dependent on me the way your mother was. And I will spend time with Bobby, be a good father."

He paused, then said, in a lower voice, "I know I can never really make it up to you, son, for those years, but I'd like to try. For so long, you wouldn't let me. It was always your uncle that you turned to when you needed anything." He stopped for a moment, then said, "I never knew why you quit Georgia Tech and went to live with him."

Jeff debated only a few moments. Perhaps now was the time to tell his father about his past at Tech. "It wasn't just that I didn't like engineering," he said. He walked over to his father. "Let's get another beer."

****

The next morning—Sunday, Sandy's phone buzzed. It was Jeff. "The Durango still runs," he said.

"Want to go for a ride?"

"Yes. Come over." Sandy dressed quickly in cutoff jeans and a T-shirt and went down to the kitchen where her mother was eating breakfast. "Mom," she said, "I'm going for a ride with Jeff. I won't be long."

"I wish you wouldn't go. Some of the roads may still be a mess out there."

"Jeff's a good driver."

Sandy quickly drank a glass of orange juice and went out to the porch. When Jeff's SUV pulled up at the curb, she ran down the sidewalk, pulled open the passenger door, and got in. They gave each other a quick kiss. As she turned to fasten her seat belt, she saw her mother at the window looking out at them, her lips pinched tightly together. Sandy tried to forget that look as Jeff drove through town toward Milledge Avenue.

"How is your cut?" she asked, seeing his bandaged hand on the wheel.

"Just five stitches. It should heal fast. The nurse said you'd done a good preliminary job."

They came to his father's house and paused by the driveway to look over at the garage. Jeff said, "Would you believe everything in the apartment is still there—the refrigerator, couch, my clothes—just wet."

"But no roof. Where will you live now?"

"My father will schedule workmen to come and put on a new roof, but that will probably take a while. They'll put a tarp on it. I'm moving into his house for now. Actually, the storm turned out to be good for our relationship."

He drove on, then swung off into a little street-side park. The grass was still littered with branches and a swing set had toppled onto its side. Jeff turned off the ignition. "Dad and I had a long talk last night. You were right—I'd never heard his side of the story. I hadn't wanted to hear it. I'd just accepted what my mother told me. And he hadn't tried to talk with me about it all these years. He said he didn't want to say anything bad to me about my mother. But last night I asked him about the divorce."

"What did he say?"

"He said there were no other women. But when he had to work in his office so many nights on his book and go on those research trips, my mother got suspicious. She didn't believe he was working all that time. She started drinking. That last year my mother was sure he was having an affair with his research assistant. He thought she'd gone kind of crazy."

"So it wasn't all his fault," said Sandy.

"No. But he admitted he'd stayed away too much—in fact, he took a lot of the blame. I think I understand now what happened. My mother was insecure and emotionally dependent. She needed too strong a tie, couldn't give my father any freedom. She should have had more of a life of her own. I'm sure that's why he wanted Glenda to be part of that excavation team in Israel if she wanted to go. My dad and she love each other, but it can't mean abandoning all their other interests. They have to trust each other." He looked at Sandy. "That's the kind of 'variety' a marriage should have."

Sandy put her hand on his. "Yes."

"And I told him some things about my past too," he said. "It was what I wanted to tell you yesterday, but never got to with the tornado coming up like that." He started the car. "We can talk about that tonight."

"I told Bill I'd see him tonight." She saw Jeff's hands tighten on the steering wheel. "This has nothing to do with variety. I'm going to tell him about us."

****

Sunday night in Bill's sports car, Sandy found him intense. "I want you to stop going out with Jeff. I want *us* to be a couple."

"He and I are a couple now."

"Give me a chance. I've known you so long, and this summer I realized you're the only girl I've ever felt anything for."

"Surely you've been with girls at the University of North Carolina."

"It wasn't the same with any of the girls there. When I first saw you again after those four years away, I knew you were the one...the one I should marry. But I want to wait for marriage before...you know...sleeping together. That's special to me. It's the guys who don't want to wait that you have to watch out for."

"I don't think that's necessarily true."

"So have you and Jeff...?" He did not finish his question, but she felt he knew the answer. He finally said, in a choked voice, "You've just met him. You don't know anything about him." He looked over at her. "You know it won't last, don't you?"

Sandy's heart skipped a beat at that, but she made herself answer in a calm voice. "Right now, I just know he's the one I want to be with."

"Sandy—I need to tell you something about him."

"And I don't want to hear it, Bill. You'd better take me home."

He abruptly turned around in a parking lot and headed back toward her house. His expression was grim, almost angry. "I'd be better for you, Sandy. Your mother thinks so, too."

Anger replaced her anxiety. "How do you know what my mother thinks? I hope you and she didn't discuss this!"

"Just a little, last night before you came downstairs. She didn't say much, but I could tell how she felt." He pulled up in front of her house. "We both worry about you with Jeff. It's not just that we think this won't last…"

"Why else should you worry?"

Bill hesitated. "For one thing, he has a temper. He may physically hurt you. Remember how he was even as a kid."

Her anger notched up higher. He was sounding just like her mother, expressing unfounded, outdated fears. "It was years ago that he got in those fights. He's not like that now. I'm sorry, Bill, but I think it would be better if you and I don't see each other for a while." She got out of the car and slammed the door.

Bill started to pull away, then stopped, lowered the window and called out to her. "Just remember, if you ever need me, I'll be here."

Her mother met her at the door. "You're home sooner than I thought. Is everything all right?"

"Mom, did you and Bill discuss my relationship with Jeff last night?"

"Why—not exactly, no," said Mrs. Harris. "Sandy, what is it? Let's sit down and talk."

Sandy sat in a living room chair. ""Bill said you didn't like me going out with Jeff. He said you thought he'd be better for me. Mom, I'm twenty years old. I can judge who is right for me!"

"Like your aunt Mary did?"

Sandy opened her mouth to retort, but her mother reached out and took her hand. "I'm sorry, I shouldn't have said that. I haven't found anything more about Jeff at Tech. But there's something else about him I should tell you, something I know firsthand. It might explain why Bill feels so upset about you going out with Jeff. And it's one of the reasons why I worry about your relationship with him."

"What is that?"

"Remember those fights Jeff got in on the playground? Well, there was one boy he beat up pretty badly, but not on the playground. Do you know who that boy was?"

Sandy stared at her mother. "Who?"

"It was Bill."

****

Sandy lay in bed, half-asleep. Images moved through her mind. Of a sweet, tall giraffe munching on leaves from the treetops—Bill. Of a beautiful, stalking tiger—Jeff. The tiger leaping upon the giraffe. Of blood. She woke up with a start.

She tried to call Jeff, but the call went to voice mail. "This is Sandy," she said. "Call me."

"Why didn't I—or anyone—know that about that fight between Jeff and Bill?" Sandy had asked her mother.

"Bill didn't want anyone to know. He told everyone he'd had an accident on his bike. When I guessed what had really happened, Bill begged me not to go to the principal. The fight was after school. There must have been something between them—I never did find out what. Neither boy would say. But apparently, they met one afternoon in an empty lot." She paused. "During that fight, Jeff broke Bill's arm."

Horrified, Sandy said, "I remember when Bill had that broken arm. He was badly bruised too, had a black eye. He did say he fell while riding his bike. How did you find out what really happened?"

"Bill's parents believed him about the bike accident, but his story just didn't add up to me, so a few days later I asked him some questions about those injuries. He finally told me about the fight. Then I called Jeff in after school. That was the day you walked in on us. Jeff admitted he'd been the one to hurt Bill but wouldn't tell me anything else. Because Bill was so against anyone knowing, and because it was not on school grounds, I agreed not to go to the principal. But I made Jeff promise not to fight with anyone again or I would." She paused. "He never did."

"Jeff was in a bad psychological state then because of his parents. Their divorce must not have been long after that."

"I'm sorry to tell you what he did to Bill."

"I'm glad you did," said Sandy. "It's good for me to know."

"About your relationship with Jeff," said Mrs. Harris. "There is love and there is infatuation. Love is over time. Infatuation is sudden, ignores good judgment, and doesn't last. Your aunt Mary learned that after she eloped with a stranger after only three weeks. Jeff's like that stranger—very good-looking, appealing. But you've just met him. I know what Jeff was all those years ago. We don't know what he may have been involved with since."

"It's true he and I haven't been together long. But

he's changed since fifth grade, for heaven's sake. I think I do know him, and over time I'll get to know him even better. You must really have a talk with him soon, Mom. Then you can see for yourself how he is now."

"Perhaps." Her mother did not sound convinced,

For all her defense of Jeff, as Sandy had climbed the stairs to her room that night, she wondered if she had been unfair to Bill. And when Jeff did not call her back, she also remembered the dark-haired girl.

****

Early Monday morning, Jeff, sleeping in the guest room of his father's house, heard a text ding. He reached groggily for his phone on the table beside his bed and looked at the time. Seven thirty. Usually he was up before six on the farm, seven here in Athens. But he knew the university had cancelled classes until noon while power was being restored all over town and roads cleared. Both his classes were in the morning, so he had a free day. It seemed that even Bobby and his father were still sleeping.

The text was from his mother. —*I heard about the tornado. I am so worried. Are you okay? Why haven't you written or called?*—

He tapped the green telephone icon right away. When she answered, he said, "Hi, Mom."

"Jeffrey! We've been so worried. The news is full of stories about the tornado."

He decided it would be better not to tell her about the roof being blown off his apartment. "Everything is okay. I'm okay."

"Thank God! I couldn't sleep all night. Are you sure you're all right? I know how you are. You wouldn't admit being hurt."

125

"I'm fine, Mom. Look, my classes were cancelled for today. Why don't I come over and see you and prove it?"

"That would be wonderful. When do you think you'll get here?"

"I can leave pretty soon. I'd get there about ten. Would that work for you?"

"I'll be here. I don't work today."

"I'll see you then." Jeff clicked off and lay back in bed for a moment. He needed a shower. He wondered what had happened between Sandy and Bill last night, and what he might have told her. Just before going to sleep the night before, he'd listened to Sandy's voice mail asking him to call. There had been something strange in her voice, and somehow, he didn't feel up to responding. He didn't trust Bill. He'd only seen him a couple of times since fifth grade, but that had been enough.

Within a few minutes, showered, a cup of coffee in hand, Jeff wrote a note to his father and headed to the Durango. As he drove along Route 316, his thoughts turned again to Sandy. She'd said she was going to tell Bill about their relationship last night, but instead, he might have won her back. He had those blond, aristocratic good looks, his family had money, her mother much preferred him. And he may have told Sandy some things about his past that he himself wanted to tell her. But surely Bill had not done that. It would mean exposing something about his own past—and maybe present, as well.

He shook his head to get rid of those thoughts. He had to concentrate on his upcoming visit with his mother.

Within an hour, he reached the outskirts of the Atlanta suburb where he'd lived through his middle and high school years with her and his grandparents—and where they still lived. He pulled into the familiar driveway. The door opened as he stepped onto the porch. His mother rushed out and hugged him tightly. "Hello, sweetheart!"

He put his arms around her and kissed her cheek, then stepped back and looked at her—slim and much shorter than he, still attractive, still vulnerable looking. She had on red lipstick, mascara, and blue eyeshadow. Her brown hair hung loose around her face, and she wore a long, patterned skirt with a silky V-neck blouse. Behind her came his grandfather, a stooped man with gray hair and a little mustache, and his grandmother, with her sparkling, blue eyes and white hair still worn in a bun. They hugged him in turn.

"Come in," said his grandmother. "We've eaten, but your mother hasn't, and she's making a breakfast for the two of you."

"More of a brunch," his grandfather added. "A big one."

"We'll have pancakes and eggs and bacon. Remember those big breakfasts your grandmother and I used to make for you on weekends when you were in high school?"

Jeff wasn't very hungry, but he mustered enthusiasm. "I sure do. And that sounds great."

"We'll talk to you later," said his grandmother, squeezing his hand. "I think your mother wants you to herself for a bit."

As she and his grandfather headed toward the television room, his mother led him to the kitchen. She

127

had already mixed up the pancake batter, and now she began ladling half cups of it onto a griddle. "So tell me all about your life at the university."

Jeff told her about his classes, the gym, swimming pool. Then she turned to the subject of his garage apartment. "I hope you don't have to see much of your father while you're staying there. I know he upsets you. And now he has that child, too. Is the child a bother?"

"Not at all." Then Jeff knew what he had to say. "Mom, there's something I want to tell you about Dad."

Her mother paused apprehensively in her work at the stove. "Oh? What's that?"

"We had a talk last night after the tornado. He told me he *wasn't* having affairs before the divorce."

"Of course he'd say that."

"I think he really wasn't. And he said something else. He blamed himself for being away so much. He said he hadn't been a good husband or father, that his new wife and Bobby were his second chance."

"He said that?" She turned and looked at Jeff a long moment, then turned slowly back to the stove. Her hand grasped the spoon and she absently re-stirred the remaining pancake batter. "I suppose I wasn't the ideal wife either, was I?"

Chapter Nine

Dr. Hudson called Sandy early on Monday, saying he wanted her to come and sit for Bobby even though he wouldn't have to teach that morning. She should come around noon, and he would stay at his office later, until about six. Sandy spent the morning editing the photos she had taken of the storm. She sent them to the local paper, *The Banner-Herald.* Perhaps they could use some of them.

When she arrived at the Hudson's, a work crew was just finishing putting a tarp over the roof of the garage. Jeff's SUV was gone.

"Hello, Sandy," Dr. Hudson greeted her. "The electricity is back on. Jeff can put his apartment back in order now that the tarp is in place. So things are getting back to normal."

"Where's Jeff?"

"He went to see his mother and grandparents and will be back later today." He looked at her a little quizzically, as if to say, "You didn't know?"

"Oh, I see," Sandy said, embarrassed that she had asked. "Hi, Bobby!" She turned to the little boy as he came running to her.

But all afternoon, she wondered why Jeff hadn't called. The Durango turned into the driveway at a little before five. He parked and she saw him look at her car and hesitate. Then he got a bag of groceries out of his SUV and came to the back door. She opened it for him.

"You're still here," he said.

"Yes. Were you hoping to avoid me?"

"No, of course not." She stepped aside as he came in and set the grocery bag on the counter. "I've been working in the library. Then thought I'd pick up some groceries for my dad while I'm staying at the house."

"You didn't call me."

"I wanted to give you plenty of time."

"Time for what?"

"To see Bill. To hear what he had to say. To think."

"I didn't need time to think."

"I wanted you to be sure."

"I *am* sure. I won't be seeing Bill for a while."

"Only a while?"

"You forget that he and I have been friends since we were babies. Our parents are friends. I'm sure I'll see him sometimes." Her voice lowered. "But there will never be anything between us like what's between you and me. How could there be?" She took his hand. "I told him that."

"And what did he say?"

"Nothing. Nothing important."

Jeff looked down at her for a minute, then nodded.

Bobby dashed in from the living room where he'd been watching a DVD. "Jeff!"

"Hi, buddy!" Jeff picked up the little boy. "What's happening?"

"I'm watching a movie about Spiderman. I put it on pause."

The look of pride on Bobby's face made her laugh.

"Kids are technically skilled today."

"Better than we were." He set Bobby down. "Buddy, I have to put these groceries away. Go back and watch the movie, and in a minute, I'll come in and watch it with you. Okay?"

"Okay."

They watched him run back to the living room. Jeff put his arms around Sandy, and she leaned against him. "You visited your mother?"

"Yes, she'd heard about the tornado and was worried. So I went over to see her and my grandparents. She's okay now."

"Your father said you could get the apartment back in shape now that the tarp is over the roof."

"The workmen won't be able to replace it anytime soon, but the tarp should keep the apartment dry." He smiled down at her. "We can still have picnics there."

It was only on her way home that Sandy remembered: Jeff had wanted to tell her something the night before. And now she needed to ask him about that fight with Bill.

****

But everyday life, everyday duties, filled their time—school, babysitting. The paper had used some of her photos in the coverage of the storm, and she was thrilled when people—including Jeff—complimented her. "These are good," he said. "I'd hardly realized you were taking them!"

On Wednesday, when Sandy got home from the Hudsons, her mother met her at the door. "Your aunt Mary is here."

"Oh. I didn't know she was coming."

"It was sort of a surprise. She drove up from

Brunswick. She wanted to check on us after the tornado. She's spending the night."

"How wonderful," said Sandy, still wondering at the sudden visit.

Her mother beckoned her inside. "She's in the living room."

Aunt Mary sat on the couch, a glass of what looked like a scotch and water in her hand. She put it on an end table and came forward to hug her niece. "Hello, Sandy." She was a tall, slender woman with ash blonde hair in a twist and red lipstick. She drew back and examined her. "My, you look so pretty."

"So do you."

"She looks more like she's your daughter than mine, Mary," Mrs. Harris said. "How did babysitting go today, honey?"

Sandy set down her heavy tote and sank into an upholstered chair. "It was fine."

"Mary and I had a good talk this afternoon," said her mother. "It's so much better in person than on the phone. Now it's your turn. I need to go to the kitchen and get dinner started. Would you like a drink?"

"No, I'm good." Sandy watched her mother leave the room.

Aunt Mary sat back down and picked up her glass. "I hear you've got a new boyfriend."

"Is that how my mother put it?"

"I guess it's what I interpreted." She smiled in a friendly, girl-to-girl way. "Tell me about him."

"There's not much to tell."

"I don't believe that. Your mother said this is quite sudden. That he's the son of the professor you're working for."

"Yes."

"Well, what does he look like?"

"He's pretty big, strong. He has dark hair, a cleft in his chin, hazel eyes…They look gold sometimes."

"He sounds good looking."

"He is."

"Your mother thinks you're getting pretty deeply involved with him."

Sandy wished she'd accepted a drink. Her mother didn't mind if she had a gin and tonic, wine, or a beer once in a while.

"You know what happened to me all those years ago," said Aunt Mary. "I thought I was in love. Greg was so handsome. He had dark hair too, but his eyes were blue. He made me feel—I can't describe it even now. Like all the love songs."

Sandy's heart began to beat faster. Her mother must have arranged this. Yet she knew exactly the feelings her aunt was describing. "Greg…I never knew his name."

"We ran away together. I was about your age— nineteen, old enough to get married without parental consent. At first, it was perfect. We lived on the beach, walked in the sand, swam in the ocean, just carefree. He played guitar and sang at some of the beach bars. I had false identification so I could be served. We probably drank more than we should have. But then the money ran out and he changed."

"I know how he changed," Sandy said. "Mom told me all about it."

"All?" Aunt Mary stared at her, and her eyes filled with tears. "I had no idea that Greg would hit me, throw things at me, push me down the stairs. I had to call the police. I was pregnant. I lost the baby. I wasn't able to get pregnant again."

"I know why you're telling me this, Aunt Mary."

"I just want you to be careful, honey."

"I'm not going to elope with Jeff."

"But you may fall in love with him, have sex with him. That can hurt you, too." Her aunt paused. "Your mother told me what Jeff was like in her class."

"Mom can't seem to get over that," said Sandy. "But it was years ago. Jeff told me about it. His parents were having problems."

"Not all kids whose parents have problems beat up other children."

"Not all boys who fight as children grow up to abuse their girlfriends or wives."

Aunt Mary gave her a searching look. "You *are* in love with him."

Sandy stood. "I'm glad you've come to see us. And I think you've had the conversation with me that my mother wanted you to have. Now let's just enjoy the rest of your visit. I think I'll go get a drink after all. A real one." She picked up her tote and left the room.

Aunt Mary did not return to the subject again. The next morning, before leaving the house, Sandy stopped by the door of the guest bedroom where her aunt sat at the dressing table pinning her hair up into its twist. "I wanted to say goodbye. I have a class."

"Goodbye, Sandy. I'm sorry if I overstepped last night. I only said what I did because I love you. And your mother is so worried. But I've been thinking. Love is not always wrong. What happened to me was probably just bad luck."

Sandy reached out and touched her aunt's hand. "I

am so sorry about what happened to you, Aunt Mary. I promise I'll be careful."

But later Sandy thought, *I can't let this go on. Surely if Jeff and I just sit down and talk with Mom, she'll see how great he is now.*

****

Jeff, in fact, texted her that morning. —*I thought maybe I could come over and visit you and your mother this evening. Then you and I can go out—*

At supper she said, "Mom, Jeff and I are going out tonight, but he wants to come by and visit with you first."

Mrs. Harris looked at Sandy for a long moment. Perhaps she felt she had no choice. "All right," she finally said.

At seven thirty, Jeff's SUV pulled into their driveway, and shortly after, the doorbell rang. Sandy answered it. He wore khaki slacks and an open-necked cotton shirt. He looked, Sandy thought, very handsome, with his dark hair, hazel-gold eyes, and broad shoulders. She herself was wearing a long, slim skirt, sleeveless jersey, and earrings that dangled through her long hair.

"Mom's in the living room," she said, and led him into the house.

"Hello, Jeff," said Mrs. Harris. "Come and sit down."

Jeff sat on the couch. Sandy sat beside him. "I was sorry to hear about Mr. Harris," he said.

"Thank you. Yes, it was hard—it was so sudden. But we're managing." Mrs. Harris smiled tightly. "I want to hear what's happened to you since you were in my class."

"I'll give a condensed version."

"I know when you left Athens you lived with your mother and grandparents in Atlanta. And you went to Georgia Tech for two years," she said.

"That's the first part," said Jeff. "To continue the story, when I finally realized I wasn't interested in engineering, my mother's brother, invited me to work for him. He has a CSA farm in North Carolina."

"CSA?"

"It stands for Community Supported Agriculture. He raises fruits and vegetables to sell to the community and local restaurants by subscription. He's also got a small herd of dairy cows and a couple horses."

"So that's why you left Tech? You realized you weren't interested in engineering?"

"Right. I lived on his farm for two years and loved it. My uncle has no children. He told me he wanted me to take over the farm someday and said he'd pay my expenses if I went back to school at UGA and got my degree in the College of Agriculture and Environmental Sciences. So here I am, starting with summer classes." He shrugged a little. "That's it."

"Well," Mrs. Harris said, "I'm glad you've found something you want to do. Of course, farming isn't easy. Government policies, the weather, all so unpredictable."

"That's true," said Jeff.

"Life is unpredictable everywhere," said Sandy.

There was a pause in the conversation.

"I thought we'd go to the Sixty Watt tonight," Jeff said. "There's a good band playing there."

"Yes, Thursday nights are a big night for the college students, aren't they?" said Mrs. Harris. "I always wondered about their Friday morning classes."

"I have one," said Jeff. "We won't be too late." He rose. "It's good to see you again, Mrs. Harris. I never forgot you."

"And I never forgot you," she replied.

****

In the safety of the SUV, Jeff and Sandy kissed at last. He turned on the ignition and backed out of the driveway. "We can leave the Sixty Watt early."

"I think it went well, don't you?" she asked.

"You mean my *interview* with your mother?"

"I hate to call it that, but yes," she said. "I learned something about you myself. I didn't know that your uncle wants you to take over the farm."

"That will just be someday. But when I get my degree, he wants me to come back and be his partner."

"That would be wonderful," Sandy said. "North Carolina is a beautiful state."

Jeff glanced over at her. Although he'd told Mrs. Harris the truth, it wasn't the whole truth. "I think your mother still doesn't know what to make of me," he said. "That's not too surprising. I was a real problem for her back when she was my teacher. Bill was her favorite. I'm sure he still is."

"She'll have to get over that," said Sandy. "But Jeff, there *is* something I've been wondering about." He gave her a quick, apprehensive look. "My mother said something about…you and Bill. She said you and he had a terrible fight that year in her class, not on the playground. You hurt him pretty badly."

"Self-defense."

"You were so much stronger than Bill. You didn't have to break his arm!"

Jeff's face darkened. "I don't want to talk about it."
They had reached downtown Athens. Seeing a parking
space, he suddenly swerved, then parked quickly,
skillfully. "Come on." They got out of the SUV.

Under the marquee of the Sixty Watt, Jeff paid the
entry fee, and their hands were stamped. As soon as
they entered the building, loud music enveloped them.
They could not have talked any more if they'd wanted
to.

****

They were back in Jeff's apartment after leaving
the Sixty Watt. Above them, the striped tarp stretched
like a circus tent as they lay together, warm, happy in
the afterglow of passion. Finally, Sandy stirred. "I
should get home."

"I should get you home." Neither moved for a
while. Then Sandy sat up. "My mother stays awake
until I'm back. She can't help it. It will be better in the
fall when I move into an apartment with Kathy."

"We're too old to live with parents. But my dad is
pretty cool." He sat up and reached for his shirt. "I just
remembered—he wants me to ask you to dinner at his
house Saturday. Bobby will be with us, of course.
Would it be too much like babysitting?"

"Oh, no, I love Bobby."

"Dad says he has a shrimp dish he makes for
company."

"I can bring a salad."

"I'll tell him."

They finished dressing. Jeff turned off the lamp
beside the bed, and they made their way down the
stairs. He still had not told her about his past at Tech.
His father had accepted that pretty well; his confession

had actually strengthened their bond. But how would Sandy react? Somehow, that night he hadn't wanted to talk about it. Maybe it was because of seeing her mother. Or her asking him about the fight with Bill. Or maybe he just could not bear the possibility of ruining their magical evening and a relationship he was coming to value more and more.

****

Although Sandy had not yet found out about Jeff's fight with Bill or about what he'd wanted to tell her that day before the storm, another long-standing issue was solved that week. Saturday night, as the Hudsons and Sandy sat around the dining room table, the relationship between Bobby and Jeff finally had to be confronted, for the little boy suddenly asked, "Is Jeff my uncle?"

Sandy was passing the rolls, and froze for a second, then asked, "What makes you think that?"

"Jimmy and George's uncle came to the pool with them yesterday. He played with them in the water. He's big like Jeff."

"Oh, I remember that," said Sandy.

Jimmy and George were the two brothers Bobby played with at the pool. The day before a man had come with them and their mother, who introduced him to Sandy as her brother.

Dr. Hudson said, "No, Bobby, Jeff is not your uncle."

"You know what Jimmy and George are to each other, don't you?" asked Sandy.

"They are brothers," said Bobby.

Jeff put his hand on Bobby's arm. "I am *your* brother."

Bobby looked at Jeff in disbelief. "You're too big."

139

"He is your big brother," said Sandy. "Brothers come in all sizes."

"But brothers live together. Jeff just came here."

A long moment of silence followed. Then Professor Hudson spoke. "I am Jeff's father, too. But sometimes there is a first mommy and a second mommy. Jeff's mommy was the first. He has been living with her. Your mommy is the second. She lives here, with us. She'll be back soon."

"Where is Jeff's mommy?" Bobby asked.

"She lives in Atlanta," said Jeff. "I've come here to go to school. And I wanted to meet you—because we are brothers."

Bobby was thinking. "I like having such a big brother," he said after a moment. "I can jump off your shoulders in the pool."

"Yes, you can," said Jeff.

This was enough for the three-year-old. Bobby smiled widely and went back to eating.

****

The summer weeks slipped by. Sandy and her mother finished the sad duty of packing up her father's clothes and giving them to charity. Mrs. Harris went through his papers, pouring over them at his desk every night, clicking on his computer screen, sometimes conferring with Sandy or sharing things she found.

Sometimes Sandy brought Bobby to visit his grandmother, who was getting around better with her new knee. The roof on Jeff's apartment was rebuilt.

She and Jeff saw each other as often as possible. He met her at the pool, where he continued teaching Bobby to swim. On weekends, they went kayaking and hiking and spent time in his apartment. Sandy, with her photographer's eye, etched many images from these days deep in her heart: Jeff on the Broad River in the kayak beside her, his dark hair wet and curling slightly in the sun...hiking ahead of her on a mountain trail with a backpack on his strong back...lying beside her on the sofa-bed in the apartment, hands behind his head.

They now avoided, it seemed by mutual unspoken consent, the subjects they once had tried to face. Jeff thought: Is there any need to tell her about my drug dealing? Why would she have to know? Sandy thought: Why should I ask him about his fight with Bill? It would be opening an old wound. Let the past stay past.

They were in an idyllic bubble of time, one they did not want to burst. But of course, then it did, as bubbles do.

Chapter Ten

On the last Friday of the summer session, Jeff
unlocked his apartment door and swung it open. As his
eyes adjusted to the dim light, he realized a thin, dark
figure was sitting at his kitchen table, one he
remembered from many meetings in the abandoned
Atlanta factory. He stood still a moment, then slowly
moved into the room.

"Hello, Jeff," the familiar voice said. "You didn't
let us know you were back in Georgia."

He dropped his backpack on the floor, reached
over, and flicked on the light. "How did you get in here,
Elgin?"

"These locks are easy to pick."

Jeff sat down on the other kitchen chair. "You been
waiting long?"

"Not too long. I looked up your schedule."

"What do you want?"

"To offer you your old job. I think you'd be good
at dealing here at UGA."

God, this was the nightmare he'd been afraid of.
But he kept his voice level. "Not interested."

"You should be. You'd make a lot of money. More
than at Tech, I think. And we need you."

"Sorry. No way."

"Be smart, Jeff, you were good at this. It was just

142

bad luck the police stopped you. But your record is only for possession, so there'd be no problem here at UGA. Unless someone informs the administration about your...past career."

"Who's going to do that?"

Elgin sat back in the chair, then, grinning, at ease, "I think Student Affairs might want to know about your activities at Tech. The ones not on your record."

Jeff wanted to wrap his hands around the man's skinny little neck. "Get out of here, Elgin."

The tall, thin man rose casually, as if he had nothing more serious on his mind. "Think about it. In a few weeks, students will arrive for the fall semester with a big demand for products—grass, THC oil, Xanax, Adderall, maybe even some coke. I'll supply, you'll sell. We'll split sixty-forty, just like before. I have a phone and a list of contacts for you." He pulled out a folded sheet of paper and a small cell phone. He placed the phone on the table.

Jeff stood too and batted the paper to the floor. "I said I'm not interested."

Without taking his focus off Jeff, Elgin picked up the paper and laid it carefully on the table beside the phone. "We want you back in the loop, Hudson. Your clients will call you on this phone. Take good care of it. We haven't activated it yet. We'll let you know when we do. I'll be in touch."

Elgin brushed past Jeff on the way to the door. Then he was outside, and Jeff heard his footsteps going down the stairs.

Shit. How had they found him? Jeff picked up the phone and walked to the garbage can, then paused. That was not the place to dispose of a phone. He went to the table beside his bed and stuck it in the back of the drawer under a sheaf of papers. Then he went to the refrigerator and pulled out a can of beer. Popping it open, he slumped in his chair at the kitchen table and took a long swallow. Who would have good reason to find Elgin and tell him where he was?

He could think of only one person.

****

That evening, Sandy sat beside Jeff in the big circular booth at Ruggeri's with the usual group. Jeff seemed distracted, and she was about to ask him if he wanted to leave when they saw Bill at the bar. He looked over at them and seemed about to turn away. Then he changed his mind and sauntered over, carrying his mug of beer.

"Hi, Bill," Sandy said, trying to sound friendly.

"We haven't seen you in a while," said Kathy. "Come sit with us."

Sandy felt her nerves tingle as Bill sat down at the end of the booth across from Jeff and set his mug on the table. "So how is college treating you?" he asked, eyeing Jeff. "What is it you're studying? Farming?"

"I'm in the College of Agriculture and Environmental Science."

"Oh, fancy name." Bill spoke loudly, the hostility in his voice barely repressed. "I heard you've already worked on a farm. Why do you need to come back to school?"

Sensing the tension at that end of the table, the rest of the crowd stopped talking. Jeff answered, "One reason is to learn new farming techniques."

"Such as?"

"Ones that are environmentally better...Here in

144

Georgia, planting no-till cotton in last year's corn stubble. Injecting manure into the soil to reduce runoff from the fields." He paused, shot Bill a glance. "Using more natural pesticides—instead of the kinds that you sell in your store."

"You're saying our store shouldn't sell pesticides?" Bill's tone was overtly hostile now.

"Pollinators are dying out because of the kinds of pesticides a lot of farmers—and gardeners—use. There are better ways."

"And so you're going to get this degree and change the world?"

Jeff reached toward his beer mug, but—was it on purpose?—knocked it over. The beer ran across the table and dripped onto Bill's lap. Bill got out of the booth quickly, snatching a napkin. "Sorry about that," said Jeff, in a tone that wasn't sorry. He looked up as Mrs. Ruggeri ran to the table with her large dish towel and began wiping the table.

"I'll get you another beer, honey," she told Jeff.

"I think we'd better go," Sandy said quietly.

"That's all right, Mrs. R," Jeff said. "We were just leaving." He and Sandy slid out of the booth.

Bill, standing there dabbing at his pants with a napkin, turned angrily and spoke so that only Jeff and Sandy could hear. "Do you want a rematch?"

Jeff turned and glared at him. "What do you mean—a rematch?"

"Another round of that fight we had in fifth grade."

"You know, I'd really like that. When it's just the two of us."

As Jeff guided Sandy toward the door, Bill followed them. "It would be more equal this time."

"I sure hope so." Jeff opened the door for Sandy and walked out behind her. Bill watched them go.

They'd reached Jeff's car when they heard footsteps coming toward them fast across the pavement. Bill's tall shadow loomed in the lights as he grabbed Jeff's arm. "How about now?"

Jeff jerked his arm away. "If that's what you want." He reached in his pocket, pulled out his car keys and wallet, and handed them to Sandy. "Get in the car, behind the wheel."

Her hand closed around what he had handed her. *This was crazy.* "No—Jeff, Bill—"

Before she could get anything more out, she heard a *thunk*, then another as Bill swung his fist first into Jeff's jaw, then into his solar plexus. Jeff, barely ready to fight, doubled over. Bill stood back and watched, a little smile on his lips. Horrified, Sandy got in the car as Jeff had directed, leaving the door open.

Jeff slowly straightened, a trickle of blood at the corner of his mouth. He looked at Bill, his eyes burning. Then abruptly he lunged toward Bill, pushing him over against the brick side of Ruggeri's. Bill faced Jeff, looking somewhat apprehensive now. Their expressions grim, the two young men moved back to the parking lot pavement, where they circled each other. It was over quickly. Jeff sprang forward, hit Bill with a right hook in the face, then a left to his ribs, then, even as the tall young man slumped forward, he dealt a hard blow to his abdomen. Bill fell flat to the ground, face down. Jeff stood above him, fists clenched, ready for more. But Bill did not move.

Perhaps someone inside Ruggeri's had seen something and called the police, because a siren began to wail, growing louder as it came closer. Jeff ran around to the passenger side of the SUV, jumped in, and slammed the door. He turned to Sandy. "Get me out of here."

Sandy, numb with shock, pulled her car door shut, turned the key in the ignition, and, tires squealing, drove out of the lot's back entrance. In the rearview mirror, she saw Bill lying there and several customers from Ruggeri's coming to the lot's front entrance. She drove fast down the street in the opposite direction, barely pausing at the stop sign at the intersection with the main road. Turning onto that road, she headed out of town. Only then did she look over at Jeff. "Where shall I go?"

"Just keep driving."

She went to the only place she could think of—the hill overlooking town where they had first made love. Reaching the site, she parked and turned to Jeff. Visions of his hard fists striking Bill brought her mother's warnings and her aunt Mary's experience crashing through her brain. Her voice trembled. "You looked so angry when you were hitting Bill. He might be badly hurt."

"Nothing time won't take care of." Jeff reached into the back seat of the car, found a bottle of water, and took in a mouthful, then opened the car door and spat it out. "He's improved his fighting techniques since fifth grade."

His breathing evened out as he became aware of Sandy's stunned expression. "I have a police record. I didn't need to be there when they got on the scene."

"Surely not from when you robbed the school in *fifth grade*?"

He didn't seem to hear. "But Bill will probably report that I was the one who beat him up." Jeff slammed the car door shut. "He always watched those fights I got into on the playground. I know he wanted to have one with me himself. But I wouldn't fight him then. He was too skinny, too weak."

"But my mother said you and he did fight—just not on the playground."

"That's right."

"You broke his arm!" She paused. "Why?"

He turned to her. "All right, if you really want to know about that." He took a deep breath, drank another swig of water. "After school, I sometimes cut through a field on the way home. Bill knew that, knew my route. That day, I was going through the field when he jumped me. I wasn't afraid of him—I knew I was stronger than he was. Then...I saw he had a knife." He paused, glanced at her. "So I had to get the knife. I had to make him drop it. That was how I broke his arm. It just happened. I threw the knife into Tanyard Branch—the creek that ran beside the field. I was so angry I hit him a few times. Then I let him get up, and he ran away."

Sandy looked at Jeff in disbelief. "When my mother called you in and asked about the fight, why didn't you tell her he had a knife?"

Jeff stared out of the windshield at the lights of the city below. "I thought she wouldn't believe me, and the knife was gone. Anyway, he stayed away from me after that. And I promised your mother I'd stop fighting." He laughed a little. "I did. I robbed the school instead." He looked back at Sandy, then focused on her intently. "It was you that day, wasn't it? You were the little girl outside your mother's classroom."

"Yes."

"I ran right into you."

Jeff began to reach out to her, but she shrank back. It was time to ask. "What about the drugs at Tech?"

"Drugs?"

"My mother found an online newspaper article about your roommate selling drugs at Georgia Tech. You were in the accompanying photograph, and the reporter said the police questioned you but found no evidence to arrest you. My mother still thinks you must have been involved with selling. Were you? Is that what this *police record* is all about?"

He opened his car door. "Okay, that's right. I've been meaning to tell you about that, too, but there's not time now. Get out—we'll change seats. I'll drive and drop you off at your house." She did as he instructed, sitting in horrified silence beside him.

As soon as he drew up to the curb by her house, she put her hand on the door handle, not looking at him. "Sandy?" he said.

"Let me know if the police contact you about the fight at Ruggeri's."

She got out of the car and ran into the house. There was a guest bathroom on the first floor, and she rushed to it, knowing she was going to be sick. The violence of Jeff's fight with Bill, Jeff's story about Bill and the knife—how could that be true?—and then his admission he'd sold drugs at Tech, never telling her all this time—it was too much. She had trusted him.

She heard her mother's voice outside the bathroom door. "Sandy? What is it?"

She flushed the toilet and wiped her mouth. "I have a little stomach thing."

149

Her mother opened the door. "Oh, sweetheart." She helped Sandy to her feet. "Has Jeff gone home?"

She nodded.

"Come on, sit down. I'll get you some Alka Seltzer." She led Sandy to a kitchen chair, worked a moment at the kitchen counter, then put the fizzy drink before her. Sandy was afraid it would make her sick again, but after drinking it, she did feel better.

"Thanks, Mom."

"Food poisoning, perhaps?"

Sandy shook her head.

"Was it something with Jeff?"

Sandy looked at her mother, surprised at her insight.

"I found something else about him on the computer tonight."

Sandy did not even ask what it was. She just waited for her mother to tell her, as of course, she would.

"I found a site on Google. You had to pay a fee to look up a person to see if he had any record of arrests or convictions, so I paid and looked up Jeff. He's been in jail in Fulton County."

"In jail? For what?"

"It was the year following that article I found. All he was charged with was possession, but I'm sure they thought there was more to it than that. They put him on probation for a year. Now we know the real reason he quit Tech and went to his uncle's farm."

****

Jeff parked his truck and stomped up the stairs to the apartment. He threw his wallet and keys on the kitchen table and slumped on his bed—where earlier he'd thought he'd soon be with Sandy. Now everything had changed. It was what he'd been afraid of—why he'd known he should not get involved with her. Her mother, that old fifth-grade teacher who had seemed to him as a kid such a monster, had become a monster again, telling Sandy about how he'd beaten up Bill, finding out about his life at Tech. He'd seen how she ran from him.

The other monster in his life had come back in the form of Elgin. The nightmare of drug dealing was about to ensnare him again.

And this very night, Bill might be telling the police a story that would send them to him even sooner.

He got up and walked to the cell-sized bathroom. In the mirror above the little sink, he peered at himself, hair wild, eyes bloodshot, the cut on his lip beginning to scab. He tasted the remains of blood in his mouth, felt the bruising in his fists. He turned on the shower, stripped off his clothes, and stepped into the cool shards of falling water. Leaning against the side of the metal stall, he closed his eyes. It seemed that Sandy was lost. Given the trouble he was about to be in, that was for the best. But in spite of everything, he wanted to keep on with his studies. He'd have to figure out what to tell the police if Bill sent them. And he'd have to decide what to do about Elgin.

Maybe it would have been better after all if he'd never come to Athens.

He remembered something then and opened his eyes. He wouldn't involve him, that he swore. But at least he'd found his father.

****

The next morning, Sandy was awakened by the buzzing of her phone.

It was Kathy, excited. "Did you hear?" she said. "Right after you and Jeff left Ruggeri's, Bill left too—and he got attacked in the parking lot. He said somebody drove up beside him, jumped out of the car, and demanded his wallet. Bill put up a good fight before the guy grabbed it."

"How is Bill?"

"He's bruised, and he'll be sore for a while. He's okay, though. The guy who attacked him must have heard people coming. Bill said he jumped back in the car and drove away. He must have dropped Bill's wallet. The police found the wallet lying beside him. Everything was still in it."

"Did the police catch the attacker?"

"Bill didn't get a very good look at him, but he said the guy was wearing a hoodie and was a big, wrestler type. Bill defended himself pretty well to hold him off as much as he did. He said the guy's car was a white Ford convertible. He was able to give the police the first part of the license number. But they didn't find a car of that description or any vehicle with those license numbers in the area."

"A Ford convertible, Bill said?"

"Right. After he talked to the police, his parents came and took him to the emergency room to be checked. They said he's okay, nothing broken, no internal injuries, only a mild concussion. You and Jeff must have left the lot just before it happened. Too bad—Jeff could have helped him. Maybe together they could have held the guy for the police."

Sandy called Jeff as soon as she and Kathy finished talking, figuring she owed him at least that. She told him what Kathy had said. "So Bill didn't give your name to anyone," she ended.

Jeff's response was strange. "Not about that, anyway." Then he said, and his tone was brusque, "Maybe we'd better not see each other for a while."

Sandy bit her lip. "I was thinking the same thing."

****

For two weeks, she did not see or talk to Jeff. When she wasn't babysitting or in class, she made meals with her mother in the kitchen; they gardened together; and on that first weekend, Sandy joined her mother's friends at a movie. The next weekend they drove to Brunswick to visit Aunt Mary and Uncle Tim. The four of them walked on the beach. Sandy did some body surfing. They had dinner in a restaurant overlooking the ocean.

On Sunday, as she and her mother were on their way back to Athens from Brunswick, Mrs. Harris looked over at Sandy from the driver's seat. "These have been a wonderful two weeks. I'm so happy to have my little girl back."

At her words, Sandy felt as though a knife twisted in her heart. She loved her mother, but she was not a little girl anymore. There was someone else she needed in her life besides her mother.

That night, she called Jeff. "I just wanted to see how you were doing. I miss you."

There was a long pause, then he said, "I miss you."

"We need to talk. Can I come over?"

After another long pause, he said, "Yes."

Sandy went to her mother's bedroom, where Mrs. Harris was getting dressed to go with her friends on a rescheduled movie night. "I can't go to the movie with you tonight after all."

"Why not?" Mrs. Harris looked at her daughter and nodded. "You're going to see Jeff."

"Yes."

The worry furrows appeared between her mother's eyebrows. But she too knows, Sandy thought, that I'm no longer a little girl, that time cannot be turned back.

When Sandy got to Dr. Hudson's home, she parked next to Jeff's Durango. Dr. Hudson's car was not there; he must have taken Bobby somewhere, perhaps to visit his wife's mother. As she climbed the stairs, Jeff opened the apartment door and waited at the top. She walked past him into the kitchen and turned to him.

"I believe you about Bill and the knife," she said. Then she was in his arms.

****

"Sandy, I want to tell you about what happened at Tech," he said as they lay together on his bed.

She touched his lips. "That's all right. I know it's over now."

"No, it's not. And you need to know."

Jeff sat up, leaning against the back of the couch, which was like the headboard. "When I got to Tech, I lived in the cheapest dorm. My dad was paying tuition, but my mom didn't have a lot of money, and I wanted to take as little as possible from her and my grandparents. I had a scholarship, but it went for books and board, so I didn't have much left over. I was assigned an upperclassman roommate who, as it turned out, was dealing drugs on campus. I didn't know that at first. He offered me some marijuana when I was stressed with the new situation and the classes at school. It helped. He told me it helped a lot of people, that it really should be legal. He said if I helped him sell

154

it to students from the supplies he had, I could make some money. So I did. Then the practice expanded. He started me selling THC oil and the prescription drugs students wanted. Together, we developed a pretty wide clientele."

Sandy felt numb. She remembered the newspaper article with the picture of the handcuffed Tech students who'd been dealing with Jeff in the background. Her mother had been right: he was involved too. "Then your roommate was arrested?" she asked.

"He and another guy were caught and expelled, but the police couldn't find anything on me. So I took over their customers. I'd meet the supplier at night in an old factory, get the merchandise, give him his share of the money."

"Were you still taking drugs yourself?"

"No, I was on the other side of the…business."

"The business"—what a term for something so horrible. She thought also of the news stories she'd read about trafficking—about dealers, including students, who had been killed by their bosses or clients. "Dealing can be dangerous," she said.

Jeff's eyes flashed. "I never want to deal again. But not just because it was dangerous for me. *Drugs* are dangerous. I could have been hurting people. Or enabling them to hurt themselves. And my supplier kept wanting me to deal even more dangerous, harder stuff."

She reached out then and took his hand. Her mother may have been right about him selling drugs— but she'd been wrong about *him*. "How did you get out of…the business?"

"One night, I'd finished my deliveries and was driving home when the police picked me up—I never knew why they stopped me. I had less than only a few grams of weed left in the car, and they didn't find any cash or the scales and packaging—I'd hidden them well. So they only charged me with a misdemeanor, but they suspected I'd been dealing. The judge set the bail as high as he could by law. I didn't want either my mother or father to know about my arrest, so I called my uncle. He came and paid my bail, got a lawyer for me, got me off with a year's probation. But when I told him the whole situation, he said I had to quit school and come back to the farm with him. The judge gave permission for that. Turned out that going to the farm was the best thing I ever did. I realized that was the kind of work I wanted to do."

"You'll never have to be involved with that supplier and his ring again," Sandy said. But Jeff remained silent. A terrible foreboding came over her. "Will you?"

"He's found me here. His name is Elgin—that's the only name I know him by. He came to the apartment a couple of weeks ago. He wants me to deal at UGA."

"*Oh, no*! How did he find out where you were?"

"That's the million-dollar question. I'd cancelled all my social media accounts, changed my email address. I'm not in touch with anyone at Tech."

"Can't you just say no to Elgin?"

"It's not that easy. He says they'll inform the UGA administration about my dealing at Tech if I don't start again. That could mean the end of my program here."

"Why don't you report *him* to the police?"

"I'm thinking of that. But Elgin's really bad, Sandy. He's dangerous. That's why you should stay away from me now."

She shook her head decisively. "I learned something these last two weeks."

"What's that?"

"I can't stay away from you."

Chapter Eleven

Together, they put a plan in place. With Sandy's encouragement, Jeff went to the Dean of Students at UGA and told the story of his drug dealing at Tech and of Elgin's attempts to make him deal at Georgia. The Dean decided to take no action about Jeff's past, but he notified the local police about the situation.

They told Jeff to go along with Elgin. He would wear a wire when they met to record as much information as possible. The hope was that, with Jeff's help, Elgin could be arrested and the others in the drug ring identified. All Jeff had to do now was wait for Elgin to contact him again and set up a meeting.

Only Sandy knew about this plan, and they were to tell no one else—not her mother, not his father, not even Jeff's uncle. As she and Jeff waited for Elgin to get in touch, they had to keep their work up in their courses and act as normal as possible. It wasn't easy. Of course, Mrs. Harris was not happy that in spite of her research results, Sandy and Jeff were back together.

In fact, she must have held hope for Sandy to think again of Bill. "I've invited the Morrisons for dinner on Wednesday," she announced not long after Sandy's reconciliation with Jeff.

"The Morrisons? Bill too?"

"Of course. You know how much I love him. He's

like a son to me."

That night, Sandy sat on her bed, her laptop balanced against her knees. She had to write a ten-page paper for her literature class. She was thinking that her topic might be "A Postmodern Theme in Jane Austen's Pride and Prejudice." She'd read a definition of postmodernism that fit her thesis: "In essence, it stems from a recognition that an individual's view of reality is not based on scientific, or objective, facts, but rather constructed to satisfy his or her own personal needs."

This is what happened to Elizabeth Bennett, Sandy thought. Without facts, Elizabeth, hurt that the aristocratic Darcy would not ask her to dance, decided he was proud and cold. She believed the story told by the soldier Wickham, who seemed to be courting her— that Darcy had cheated him out of his legacy. In reality, Wickham turns out to be a dishonest rake, and Darcy a hero. The reader, however, may also be for a time taken in by Elizabeth's beliefs.

Sandy closed her laptop, thinking. Her mother had constructed a reality about the fifth-grader Jeff. She saw him as a bad boy, a bad seed, seriously hurting Bill for no reason. Ten years later, she still saw Jeff that way, proving her point with research about his link to drugs at Tech. *Should I tell my mother that Bill attacked him with a knife?*

But her mother's reaction would probably be the same as hers at first had been. She would not believe that the sweet little Billy she'd known as a child and in grade school would do that. Now Sandy wished even more that she could tell her mother how Jeff had agreed to help the police arrest a dangerous drug supplier.

Wednesday evening after the closing hour of their

store, the Morrisons arrived for dinner. Bill was still bruised from the assault by the mysterious attacker. "Oh, how awful," her mother had said when, avoiding Sandy's eyes, he told the story of the attempted robbery in Ruggeri's parking lot.

After they'd eaten, Sandy left them all in the living room with after-dinner drinks, partially cleaned up the kitchen, then went out to the garden. She was sitting on a granite bench in the dark when the kitchen door slammed. Bill walked toward her. "I want to apologize for what happened at Ruggeri's restaurant."

She looked up at him. "Thank you for not reporting Jeff to the police."

"Well, I started the fight." After a moment of silence, he spoke again. "As a kid, I'd always wanted to fight with him. I wanted to see if now I could hold my own. And I did. At first."

"Jeff said you'd improved your fighting techniques." She thought, though it was hard to see in the dark, that Bill seemed pleased. "That was a good story you told about the hooded attacker in a *Ford convertible*."

"I was able to pull my wallet out and put it beside me just before anyone got there. That looked like the attacker dropped it."

"That was very smart of you. Sit down, Bill." Sandy moved over to the end of the bench to give him room. "I want to ask you about something else."

"Okay." A bit stiffly, as if still sore, he sat down on the bench beside her—but kept a discreet distance away. "What's that?"

"I want to know why, in fifth grade, you attacked Jeff with a knife."

"What?"

"In the field by Tanyard Branch. When you had a broken arm, you said you'd fallen on your bike. But my mother figured out that wasn't true, and then you admitted that Jeff had done it. But why did you attack him first with a knife?"

"Did Jeff say that?"

"Yes. Tell me about it, Bill. I won't tell anyone. I just want to understand what really happened, why you did it."

"Fifth grade is a hard age." Bill sat mute, then, his head down. Sandy waited.

"Okay," he said finally, "I'll tell you. I wanted to be like Jeff. All the kids looked up to him because he was so strong, so good in sports. It was almost an honor when he wanted to fight with you. He only picked the best kids to fight with." He raised his head to look at Sandy. "It was dramatic, like in the movies, two guys going after each other, rolling around on the ground, getting bloody, and when they were sent to the principal's office, both of them in trouble, it was almost like they became friends." He shifted on the bench. "So I wanted to fight with Jeff. I taunted him, I challenged him. But he wouldn't fight with me."

"But to go after him with a knife—you could have really hurt him."

"He drove me a little crazy, ignoring me, probably laughing at me inside. So I wondered how to fight him and win, even if the other kids didn't see it. We had some pruning knives in the store. I took one of the biggest, and I waited for Jeff when he came through the field. What I really wanted was just to scare that big, tough guy who laughed at me."

"You should never have done that!"

"I see that now. I should have been satisfied with what I was—a smart kid, not a fighter." He shifted uneasily on the bench. "After Jeff took the knife away and beat me up, I didn't want people to know how easily he had gotten the better of me. So I said I fell on my bike."

"How did my mother know that wasn't true?"

"I'd left my bike in the rack at school. She saw that my bike was not damaged at all. So the next day she called me in at recess and asked about it. I think, because of all Jeff's fighting on the playground, she suspected he was the one who'd broken my arm. So she kind of grilled me, and I finally admitted she was right. But I didn't tell her about my knife. And I guess neither did Jeff when she called him in. When he moved away, I'd hoped never to see him again because he knew that secret about me attacking him with a knife." He paused. "Do you hate me now?"

Sandy shook her head.

"You won't tell anyone about it, will you?"

"No. It happened so long ago. Thank you for telling me." Sandy stood up, folding her arms tight about her. "You realize you might have gotten in serious trouble back then if he'd told my mother about your knife."

Bill nodded. "I know—if she'd have believed him. So maybe I owed him one for that."

****

The university's summer courses were over. Sandy received an A on her paper on *Pride and Prejudice*, and an A in the course. Jeff earned A's in both his courses, but heard no word from Elgin.

"Maybe he's accepted your saying no," said Sandy. "Maybe he's found someone else to deal."

"But now I *want* him to contact me. I want to help put an end to that ring."

****

With the end of the summer session, Glenda was to return from her dig. "Tuesday, I will pick her up at the Atlanta airport at five o'clock," Dr. Hudson told Sandy. "Could you babysit that afternoon until we get back? We should get here about eight."

"Of course," she replied. "I know you can't wait to have her home."

That Tuesday evening, she read Bobby some of his favorite stories, but he was too excited to listen. When at last they heard Dr. Hudson's car turn into the driveway, he jumped down from the couch. "It's Mommy and Daddy!"

She followed him as he rushed to the kitchen and out the screen door. A slim, young woman who looked just as she had in the pictures, with dark hair and horn-rimmed glasses, got out of the car and ran to him. Sandy felt a lump in her throat as she watched Bobby leap into his mother's arms.

Glenda held the little boy tight for long moments as Dr. Hudson took a large duffel bag from the trunk of his car and joined them. She at last looked up and saw Sandy standing by the door. "Thank you for taking such good care of our son."

"He's a great little boy."

Bobby squirmed down from Glenda's embrace and went to Sandy. "Sandy won't go away now, will she?" he asked.

"No, she will still come to see you," said Dr.

Hudson. "In fact"—and he glanced up at the garage apartment, on which the new roof had been built—"I think you will see a lot of her."

****

Fall classes were to start in two weeks. Students were beginning to return to campus. There was still no word from Elgin. Jeff and Sandy's tension rose higher. "I wonder if he knows I've been to the police," he said.

She shook her head. "He couldn't know that."

A few days later Jeff said, "Dad wants me to go on a trip with him and Glenda and Bobby to Highlands, North Carolina, for a couple of days. It might be a good idea for me to go. I'd bring my own car. If Elgin calls or emails me to meet, I could come right back."

"It probably would be good for you to get away."

"They want me to bring you along. Would you like to come?"

"I'd love it." Then, something hit her. "What about the sleeping arrangements?"

"They won't mind if you and I share a room."

****

Mrs. Harris stood in the door of Sandy's bedroom, watching her pack for the trip to Highlands. "What time is Jeff picking you up tomorrow?"

"Around nine. We're all staying at Quinn's Lodge. We'll have a picnic with Dr. Hudson and Glenda and Bobby on the way."

Her mother continued to stand there. "You should pack a sweatshirt. It gets chilly in the mountains, even in August."

"Good idea."

The woman turned to leave, then turned back. "I know you and Jeff have gotten pretty close. Are you using birth control?"

Sandy looked at her mother, shocked.

"I was young once," said her mother.

Sandy folded another T-shirt and placed it in her duffel bag. "Jeff's being careful."

"You should set up an appointment with a gynecologist, get on the pill."

Her mother was right. She nodded. "I'll make an appointment with Dr. Miller as soon as I get back."

"It sounds like Jeff and his dad are getting along."

"They are. I just wish you liked him better, Mom."

"I only worry because there are too many 'starter marriages' today. Fifty percent of today's marriages end in divorce. When you marry, I want your happiness to last. I'd just feel better if you were in a relationship with someone I've always known and trusted. I wish…" Her voice trailed off.

Sandy went over and hugged her mother. "I want my happiness to last too, Mom."

But she knew what her mother wanted to say: "*I wish you were in a relationship with Bill.*"

****

The next day dawned warm and sunny. As they drove north, both Sandy and Jeff could feel the tension draining from them. When they turned off Route 441 onto the mountain road that led to Highlands, they saw Dr. Hudson's car ahead. "We've caught up to them," Jeff said.

His phone played its music. Sandy answered, putting on the speaker so Jeff could hear and talk too. "Hi, Dr. Hudson."

"Hi, Sandy. There's an overlook a few miles ahead. Let's stop there and have our picnic."

"That sounds good," said Jeff.

The air grew cooler as they rose in elevation on the steep, winding road. When Dr. Hudson turned off at the overlook, Jeff followed, pulling up beside him. Before them stretched a range of smoky-blue mountains. In the foreground, pink flowers bloomed on large bushes bordering a drop-off, under which was a stone cliff. It was wonderful to feel free again, to be in such a beautiful place, to be distracted from worry about Elgin. Jumping out of the car, Sandy ran toward the cliff's edge to take pictures with her phone. She was stopped only by a line of guardrails.

After walking up and down photographing the landscape, she turned and went to the picnic table where Glenda was unpacking the cooler. Jeff brought over a bag with the other supplies. "Can I have a cookie?" Bobby was asking, clambering onto the picnic table bench.

"You can have a cookie after we eat our sandwiches," said Glenda. "Sandy, do you have the napkins and paper plates?"

"They should be here," said Sandy, reaching into Jeff's bag. She distributed the paper plates and napkins and laid out a bag of potato chips, leaving the cookies out of Bobby's sight in the bag. Glenda passed out bottles of cold water and sandwiches. Everyone settled around the table.

"To our vacation and our *A* students," said Dr. Hudson, toasting with his bottle of water.

As they all raised their drinks, Bobby asked, "Who are our *A* students?" The remains of peanut butter and jelly ringed his mouth.

"Jeff and Sandy," replied Dr. Hudson. "And, of

course, your mom."

"I didn't get a grade on my independent study in Israel," Glenda reminded him. She looked at Jeff and Sandy, smiling. "But I did get an *A* from 'Dr. Hudson' when I took a course from him."

"Of course, I couldn't date her until she was no longer my student, but she was the best graduate student I ever had," said Dr. Hudson.

"Is that the reason you married her?" asked Jeff.

"There might have been a few other reasons," said Dr. Hudson.

"Can I have a cookie now?" Bobby crawled up on the table toward the paper sack.

"Here, I'll get them for you," said Sandy, and she pulled out the bag of her mother's homemade chocolate chip cookies. She handed one to Bobby first, and then passed the bag around.

"Do you bake as well as your mother does?" Jeff asked Sandy, biting into one.

"I'll have to let you judge that," she replied. "As soon as I move into my apartment, I'll make you a whole dinner. With dessert." Then she blushed, remembering what Jeff often called dessert.

"Look!" said Glenda. "A monarch butterfly!" They all turned to see the big gold-winged insect fluttering toward the bushes on the other side of the guardrails.

"How great to see one. I haven't in a long time," said Jeff.

"I'll catch it!" exclaimed Bobby, scrambling down from the table and running after it.

"No, Bobby," said Glenda. "Just look at it. You don't want to hurt it."

"Bobby, you can't catch it!" cried out Sandy—a

little panic coming to her voice. "Stay away from the edge!"

But Bobby ducked under the guardrails and reached out toward the butterfly, which lit momentarily on one of the pink-flowered bushes. And then they heard him cry out, and he disappeared from sight.

"Oh, my God!"

They all rushed to the edge of the drop-off and looked down. There was a narrow ledge about twenty feet below, covered with brush and scrub grass. Bobby lay there on his back, pale, his eyes closed. Glenda began to cry hysterically.

"I'll call nine-one-one." Dr. Hudson rushed to the car where he had left his phone. At the same time, Jeff ran to his SUV and came back with a coil of rope. He tied one end of it to a scrub tree near the edge; the other he double coiled around his waist. "I've done some rock climbing. I'll get to him."

"What will you do then?" cried Glenda.

"I'll see how badly he's hurt. If he's okay, throw down the backpack Dad and you carry him in, and I'll climb back up with him."

"And if he's not okay?"

"Then I'll be with him until we get help."

He began rappelling down the cliff, feet against the rocks. Sandy watched with bated breath. She remembered her first aid course. "Don't try to move him if he can't move himself," she called out.

"I won't," Jeff replied.

On the ledge himself now, Jeff dropped the rope, went to Bobby, and knelt beside him. "Hey, buddy," Sandy heard him say.

Bobby's eyes opened. He started to cry. Jeff ran his

hands over Bobby's arms, legs, neck. Sandy watched, now unable to hear what either said, but the little boy stopped crying and sat up.

Dr. Hudson ran back to Sandy and Glenda, his forehead furrows deeper than Sandy had ever seen them, his voice husky. "I tried to call nine-one-one. But the reception wasn't good. I couldn't get through."

"Bobby seems to be all right," whispered Sandy, a clenched fist against her mouth.

They all looked down. Bobby climbed against Jeff's chest and wrapped his arms around his neck. Jeff looked up at them.

"I couldn't get nine-one-one," Dr. Hudson called down to him.

"That's all right," Jeff called back. "I think he just had the breath knocked out of him—and got a little scraped up. He doesn't weigh much, and the bushes cushioned his fall. I'll bring him up."

Glenda ran to their car for the child carrier, then returned and threw it down toward Jeff. He reached out and caught it. He stood, put his arms through the pack straps, and positioned it on his back, then squatted down so Bobby could climb into it and ride, like a papoose, on Jeff's shoulders.

"Are you sure you can do this, son?" Dr. Hudson called.

Jeff gave a thumbs-up sign and took hold of the rope. Glenda could not watch. She sat on the ground, her hands over her face. But something in Sandy clicked into gear—the mindset she'd developed after the many photo shoots she'd gone on with John, the many pictures she'd posted on Facebook. No one could know about Jeff trying to help the police with his drug supplier, but surely seeing his rescue of Bobby on video would fully vindicate him to her mother—or to anyone who still had doubts about him.

She pulled out her phone and began shooting as Jeff rappelled slowly up the side of the cliff. As she zoomed in, Bobby looked solemn there on Jeff's back, but not afraid. Jeff, beads of sweat on his forehead, was concentrating, his feet pushing upward in a vertical step by step against the stones, his hands moving one above the other on the rope.

When he had almost reached the top, Dr. Hudson, standing at the edge, reached down, and helped him up the final few feet. On solid ground again, Jeff stepped over the guardrails, breathing heavily, but smiling. Glenda looked up and rushed to them, sobbing and embracing the little boy and his rescuer at the same time. Sandy turned off the camera. Dr. Hudson extricated Bobby from the backpack, hugged him, and handed him to Glenda. Then he turned to Jeff and, almost in tears himself, wrapped the young man in his arms.

****

The rest of the afternoon was a blur, as they brought Bobby to a doctor in Highlands who checked the little boy over, examined him for a concussion, and pronounced him fine—and very lucky. "He probably just fainted for a few minutes after the fall, but keep him quiet, don't let him watch television tonight, let him sleep normally."

Relieved, they all retired to Quinn's Lodge to rest before going out to dinner. Sandy sat on the edge of the bed in the room she shared with Jeff, looking at her phone. "I just put it on Facebook."

Jeff stood nearby in his shorts, getting ready for a shower. "What have you put on Facebook?"

"Your rescue of Bobby." Sandy held out the phone to him.

He came over to look at the little screen. "You videoed it?"

Together, they watched as it showed Jeff, Bobby on his back, rappelling slowly up the cliff, with Sandy's camera panning back to show the mountains and sharp drop-off in the background, then moving in for close-ups of the child and young man. Last came the dramatic sequence showing the young man reaching the top, the father pulling him up the last few feet, and the mother in tears, running to them and hugging both the little boy and his rescuer.

"I want my mother and all our friends to see this," said Sandy. "They don't know about what you're doing with the police. This video shows how brave you are."

She saw that flush come over Jeff's cheekbones again. "I'm not sure you should have posted it."

"Do you want me to take it down?"

He hesitated, then said, "I guess, since Elgin's found me, there's no reason to now."

****

They had dinner sitting outside under umbrellas at the Bistro Cafe on the town's main street. Glenda was still recovering from her scare, but Bobby was in high spirits, joyously recounting the ride on Jeff's back. Bandages were on his elbows and knees, and his face was scratched—the only signs of his experience. Under the table, Sandy held one of Jeff's hands, lightly stroking the rope burns on the palm.

As the waitress set the salads before them, Sandy's

171

phone buzzed. Reception here in the town, at least, was good. She looked at the name on the screen and hesitated. "It's my mother."

"Go ahead and answer," said Dr. Hudson.

"Hi, Mom."

"I saw your video on Facebook. It was amazing! Jeff was wonderful. Is Bobby all right? Is Jeff?"

"Yes, Bobby and Jeff are fine." No need to mention scratches or rope burns.

"So many people have already called us about the video. Jeff is quite a hero."

"I'm glad you think so. We all do."

"Can I speak to Jeff?"

"Sure." Sandy held out the phone to him. "My mother wants to speak to you."

Jeff took the phone. "Hello, Mrs. Harris…Yes, it was quite an experience…He was chasing a butterfly and fell. We couldn't get through to nine-one-one. I just happened to have that rope in my SUV…They do?" He shook his head. "I don't know about that."

"What?" Sandy pantomimed.

Jeff held up his hand to hush her. He seemed to be thinking for a moment. Then he spoke again to her mother. "Well, it's all right with me, if it's okay with Glenda and my father. And they would need to give Sandy credit. She took the video…All right. Goodbye."

He clicked off and handed the phone back to Sandy. "Channel Two in Atlanta wants to show your video on their local news," he said. "Someone who knows your mother and saw it on Facebook works there. But they need my permission—and yours, Sandy. They are going to call us for it on your phone in just a minute."

"I didn't expect this!" said Sandy. She couldn't help thinking: *This could be on the resume for my photojournalism career.* But letting them show the video was not up to her. "What do you think, Jeff?"

"I say yes." He now was, surprisingly, definite.

"Would it be all right with you, Dr. Hudson? Glenda?"

"I guess it would be, now that it's all over," said Dr. Hudson. "What do you think, Glenda?"

"I agree—but I still don't think I can watch it," said Glenda.

As Sandy waited for the station to call, she brought up Facebook. "Two hundred shares already!" she said of the video.

"It's going viral. You'll be giving out autographs," said Dr. Hudson to Jeff.

Sandy was still reading her phone. "Will posted a comment. He says, 'Way to go, Jeff!' She scrolled a little more. "Tom says, 'Amazing!'"

When the phone rang again, they gave permission for the television station to show the video.

****

Side by side on the bed, propped against the pillows, Jeff and Sandy watched Jeff's rescue of Bobby on the late-night news. When it was over, he turned off the television and put his arms around Sandy. "I predict you'll have a great career." He paused. "You know, I think this publicity may get something going with Elgin, if anything will. He'll think I'll be even more beyond suspicion. I'm glad I have you as my PR agent."

"And there's no charge," said Sandy. "Well, maybe one." She switched off the light.

The next morning, Jeff rolled over in bed and turned on his phone. He checked the comments on the Facebook video, which Sandy had tagged him in. "Here's something from Sheila."

I will not ask him what she says, thought Sandy.

"She says, 'Was this staged?' " Jeff smiled and shook his head. "That's Sheila for you. It's the people who spread false news who think everyone else's news is fake."

Sandy felt a lightness spread through her heart. "She spreads false news?"

Jeff looked at her. "Sometimes. Or she exaggerates. When it suits her." His phone beeped. "Uh-oh, a message just came through." He tapped the "Messages" icon.

"Who is it from?" she asked.

Jeff stared down at the screen. His voice was flat. "It's from Elgin."

Chapter Twelve

Jeff stood in a basement room at the police station while Detective Steve Terrisi, a short, dark-haired man, hooked up a tiny, black microphone to his undershirt.

"You see how it works. We'll be listening in. We have the list of contacts he gave you and that's a big help, but something else has developed. We've gotten word that Elgin's ring has expanded beyond prescription meds, marijuana, and cocaine. He's gotten involved in manufacturing and trafficking meth. He and a partner have taken over a cooking lab somewhere in this part of the state. See if you can get him to talk a little about that. Just don't make him suspicious."

"I'll see what I can do." Jeff buttoned his shirt. "This doesn't show?"

"Not at all. So you're going to meet him at Oconee Forest Park."

"Yes, at the first bench by the lake, to the left of the bridge. Eight o'clock."

"Just as it's getting dark. My partner and I will walk the area about that time too. Okay, Jeff. Good luck. We appreciate this."

And so Jeff sat on the rustic wooden bench a little before eight, looking out at the smooth, evening waters of the lake. Nighttime birds rustled and called in the trees. Then he heard footsteps coming across the wooden bridge and saw the familiar tall, stick-thin figure in a black T-shirt and jeans, a backpack on his back. Jeff sat up straight, felt his heart beat faster. Elgin hopped down the steps at the end of the bridge and turned onto the path, stopping behind the bench.

"You're right on time," Jeff said, not looking around.

"And so are you, kid." Elgin came to the front of the bench, dropped his backpack, and sat beside him. "I saw that video of you on TV. Pretty cool. I like skills like that."

"I haven't had to use them much."

"But you never know, do you? Here you go." Elgin indicated the backpack. "It's what we agreed on—a thousand grams of marijuana, twenty-five vials of THC oil, fifty tablets of Xanax, fifty of Adderall. That should be more than enough to get you through until our next meeting."

"Okay." Jeff pulled the bag to his side of the bench. "What if someone asks if I can get any…meth?"

"What, college students wanting meth? Naw, there's no demand on campus. College students aren't our clientele for that."

"I don't have to stick to college students, do I?"

"You're changing your tune, Hudson. You weren't too happy when I first asked you to deal here on campus."

"I figure if I'm in this, I'm in."

"What made you ask about meth?"

"You hear about it all the time."

Elgin studied him a moment. Then his eyes glinted. "Okay, I've started working with it. One of the pharmacists who used to supply me with pills was fired from his day job. He'd been cooking THC oil in our lab, and since he now has more time, we added meth to the menu. So we do need more dealers. You're pretty experienced—and tough. Maybe we could have you expand your dealing area—if you're interested."

"I'm interested."

"Then I may get back to you about that." Elgin pushed himself up from the bench. "I'll set up a meeting in a couple of weeks—maybe at that first football game. Bring your cash so far."

He lit a cigarette, tossed the match on the ground, and strolled back toward the bridge, smoking. Jeff sat watching. As Elgin started across the bridge, two men in shorts and T-shirts, carrying fishing poles, came across the bridge from the opposite side. Jeff knew: the promised detectives, Terrisi, the short one, and his partner, the taller, stocky one. They were supposed to have listened to the meeting, and now they would arrest Elgin. But the two men just passed him and went to Jeff's end of the bridge. Elgin crossed on to the other end and disappeared.

When the two reached the bench, Jeff stood and faced them. "What happened to the plan?"

"We decided to wait on that arrest. We want you to pursue that meth connection with Elgin."

****

Sandy stood with her mother by the front door of their house, waiting for Jeff to pick her up. Nervous, she twirled a lock of hair around her finger. Mrs. Harris patted her arm comfortingly. "I'm sure Jeff's mother will be very impressed with you, Sandy. Just remember that she *asked* Jeff to bring you over to meet her after seeing your video."

"But he told me she didn't want him to settle down yet—she thought he should date a lot of different girls. I don't know how she'll feel about me."

"I'm sure she'll be impressed with you. Here he is now. Just go there and be yourself."

Mrs. Harris had at last fully accepted Sandy's relationship with Jeff—once she saw his rescue of Bobby and his now warm relationship with his father. She smoothed the lock of Sandy's hair off her face and opened the door to wave at Jeff, waiting in his Durango parked at the curb.

I hope she won't feel as negative about me as you felt about him at first. Sandy gave her mother a quick kiss and headed out the door and down the walk to Jeff.

As they sped along 316 toward Atlanta, Sandy reached over and touched his arm. "I'm so glad this business with Elgin is over and he's in jail."

Jeff looked at her for a moment. "That's right," he said. But she thought there was a hitch in his voice. Maybe he was worried about how his mother would react to her.

"Do you have any advice for me about how to act with your mother when we get there? Is there anything I should know?"

"You already know that back before the divorce, she had drinking problems, but they're under control. She works at a makeup counter in an Atlanta department store. I showed you her picture."

"Yes. She's pretty."

"I think you'll like her—and my grandparents."

"But will they like me? Especially since I worked for your father."

"Actually, I think your video, showing Dad with

Bobby has made my mother feel better about him."

"It showed how much he cares for you, too," Sandy said. "Now that Elgin's in jail, if she likes me, everything's going to be perfect."

****

"My mother and grandparents *loved* you," said Jeff three hours later as he and Sandy were on the way back to Athens. "But I was surprised you asked Mom to come for the game next weekend and to stay at your house without checking with your mother—or me."

"Mom won't mind. She's going to Brunswick next weekend to visit Aunt Mary and Uncle Tim again," Sandy replied. "And when you mentioned that your uncle Jake was coming for the first football game of the season, I thought that would be a perfect time for her to visit too. I was so sure you'd like the idea. You do, don't you?"

"I suppose so. Anyway, she accepted the invitation. I was surprised. She hasn't been to Athens since …well, for years. I'll email Uncle Jake and tell him she'll be here." Jeff shook his head. "But, man, I didn't expect a family reunion at this game."

Back at his apartment, Jeff lay on the couch-bed, his head propped on a pillow, and tapped his phone while Sandy fixed BLTs for supper. "Well, guess what?" he said after a few minutes, reading his screen. "Uncle Jake is flying down to the game with Ash Williams, the guy who owns the land next to Uncle Jake's farm. They'll land at the Athens airport. Ash has an extra ticket he'll give to Mom so they can all sit together at the game. And he's bought a tailgate space on campus for the season."

"Oh, that's great! We can have our picnic there

before the game. Do you know this guy?"

"I've met him a couple times. He's kind of shy but all right. Never married. Has a lot of money. Loves his plane and football."

"What can I make for the tailgate? Let's see, sausage balls, pimento-cheese sandwiches, ham biscuits, stuffed eggs, shrimp dip…" Sandy approached the bed. "It can be a sort of private celebration for us."

"Celebration?"

She lay beside Jeff, leaned over, kissed him. "We'll celebrate this drug dealer problem being over."

"What about those BLTs you were making?"

She kissed him again, traced the cleft in his chin. "They can wait, can't they?"

Jeff put a hand on each side of her face and looked at her. "Okay. They can wait."

****

The Athens airport was a busy place, as it always was the day of a football game. Jeff sat behind the wheel of his Durango in the airport parking lot. Sandy was in the back seat, wearing black ankle pants, a red halter top, and sandals. Jeff's mother sat next to him in the front seat, in a bright, red dress and high heels. They had picked her up at the Atlanta-Athens shuttle earlier that morning, and now they were waiting for Ash's plane. "Will you recognize it?" Sandy asked.

"Maybe not," said Jeff. "It's a small double-engine prop like a lot of these coming in." They got out of the SUV and stood beside it, scanning the sky as one such plane after another circled, then landed and taxied down the runway, carrying in football fans from all parts of the South. "There they are!" he said suddenly, pointing to a small, white plane that attendants had just secured in a parking area. Two men had emerged from the plane door. One was a tall, solid man wearing a pilot's goggle-like dark glasses. The other Sandy recognized as Uncle Jake.

"Jake!" called out Jeff's mother, running toward them waving her arms. Sandy and Jeff followed as she rushed into her brother's embrace. Jake then gave Jeff a hug. "You remember Sandy," Jeff said, stepping back.

"I certainly do," responded Jake. "Hi, there, honey," and he hugged her too. Then he turned to the large man standing quietly nearby. "You-all, this is Ash Williams. Ash, you know Jeff. This is my sister Sibyl Tompkins and Jeff's friend Sandy Harris."

Ash stepped forward with a little smile and shook hands with Jeff, then Sandy and Sibyl.

"Sandy's got some good food ready for us," said Jeff. "I hear you've bought a spot on the campus for tailgating."

"Yes, let's get going," said Jake. "Ash, you'd better sit in the front seat, if we're going to fit three in the back."

Ash spoke then for the first time, in a slow, rumbly voice. "You just want to be between two pretty women."

Maybe he's not totally shy, thought Sandy.

Jeff's SUV joined the stream of traffic heading toward the stadium. Near the campus, it slowed down. The Georgia Bulldog colors—red and black— surrounded them as fans and students, back for the game and sorority rush even before classes started, walked along the sidewalks and across the campus. On designated grassy areas and parking lots, people were unloading cars and RVs, setting up tents, putting out picnic food. Music blared from various speakers. The whole atmosphere felt carnival-like and happy.

Directed by Ash, Jeff backed into a small, grassy space off Lumpkin Street near a large tree, turned off the ignition, and attached Ash's parking pass to the rearview mirror. Everyone got out. Jeff and Jake pulled folding lawn chairs and tables from the back of the Durango, then the ice chest and the picnic basket. Jeff handed a cold can of beer to Jake and Ash, then looked to his mother. "I have some soda."

"That will be fine," she said.

"I'll have a soda too," said Sandy, who, being underage anyway, was glad to keep her company in not drinking alcohol.

Sibyl sat in a lawn chair between Jake and Ash. Jeff and Sandy placed their chairs opposite them in a sort of circle, and once drinks were distributed, Sandy got out the appetizers she had packed. "Just save some space for the sandwiches and cookies," she told them as everyone began to dig in.

After the appetizers, drinks, and sandwiches were consumed, Sandy said, "Let's walk around. I think some of our friends are tailgating near here. I'd like you to meet them."

"Oh, that will be fun," said Sibyl.

Jeff said he was going to the porta-potties, the little portable metal buildings that served as restrooms, set up in strategic locations for every game. "Don't wait for me," he said. "I'll find you." So Jake, Sibyl, and Ash strolled around with Sandy, socializing and sampling other tailgate appetizers. But they didn't see Jeff again until they returned to the Durango to pack up and head to the stadium. He was waiting there.

"Where were you?" asked Sandy.

"I did my own socializing," said Jeff. "I couldn't find you."

Sandy thought he looked a little pale. "Do you feel okay?" she asked him, reaching up to feel his forehead.

He brushed her hand away. "I'm fine."

"Well, Sibyl and I will go on our porta-potty tour now," Sandy said.

"Don't *you* get lost," Ash told them, his laugh a throaty rumble.

As Sandy and Sibyl headed to the little telephone-booth-like structures, Ash, Jake, and Jeff made quick work of picking up trash and putting the chairs and tables into the back of the SUV. Jeff was sliding the last chair in when a man's voice called out, "Jake!" and his uncle answered, "Roy!"

Dr. Hudson stood there with Bobby. He and Jake shook hands.

"Hi," Jeff greeted them both, then hesitated. "Dad, great to see you, but you should know Mom is with us."

"Sibyl is here?"

"Yes, she's visiting Sandy for the weekend. She and Sandy have just gone over to the..." He jerked a thumb in the direction where they'd gone. "They'll be back any minute."

"Okay, right." Without saying another word, his father picked up Bobby and turned to go. But it was too late. Bobby had spotted the two women coming up the walk.

"Sandy!" he cried, squirming in delight and stretching his arms out to her.

Sandy looked up, surprised, then ran over and took Bobby from his father's arms. Sibyl, a few steps back, recognized the man standing there and stopped, frozen in place. Everyone became quiet as Dr. Hudson turned to her. "Hello, Sibyl."

"Hello, Roy." She looked at Bobby and took a deep breath. "My, what a cute little boy." Her gaze moved back to Dr. Hudson. "Doesn't he remind you of Jeff at that age?"

Dr. Hudson nodded. "Yes, he does."

"It's good of you to let Jeff live in your garage apartment."

"I was glad to help out...You're looking well, Sibyl."

"So are you."

Dr. Hudson took the little boy back from Sandy. "Well, we'd better get to our seats, hadn't we, Bobby? Mommy will be looking for us. Say goodbye."

"Bye," said Bobby. As his father carried him off, he looked back over his father's shoulder and shouted, "Go, Dawgs!"

The group laughed a little nervously and waved.

"Well," said Sibyl, in a shaky voice as the man and child merged into the crowd, "that was a surprise."

"Yes," said Jeff. "Out of eighty thousand people here, Dad comes by."

"We'd better get to our seats, too," Jake said. Ash took Sibyl's arm in an almost protective gesture, and Jake took the other. The three of them moved off toward the stadium, Sibyl, between the two men, wobbling a little in her high heels.

****

On Sunday evening, Sandy and Jeff sat at the kitchen counter in Jeff's apartment. They had taken Sibyl back to the shuttle for the return trip to Atlanta and just finished a supper of tailgate leftovers. "I think the weekend went pretty well, don't you?" said Sandy. "Even the meeting between Sibyl and your father was a good thing."

"Maybe," said Jeff.

"Sooner or later, they would have had to see each other again. And to me, it seemed they made a kind of peace." Sandy stood up to clear the dishes. "I wonder if your mother will marry again."

"She always says she's through with men."

"But she and Ash seemed to get along. I heard them say maybe they'd see each other at another football game." Sandy put the dishes in the sink and then stood there a moment in thoughtful silence.

"What is it?" Jeff asked.

"You know, Ash might be good for her. He may be quiet, but he's strong, calm, protective. She needs someone like that."

"It will just be good if they see each other sometimes at football games." He looked up at her. "So while you're analyzing relationships, what do *you* need?"

"You."

"What about your career as a photojournalist?"

She laid her hands on his shoulders. "I don't believe they're mutually exclusive."

****

When the dishes were done, Sandy turned to Jeff expectantly, but he said, "We'd better make this an early evening. There's some research I have to get done tonight."

Sandy was taken aback. "All right, I'll go on home," she said. They kissed each other quickly, and she went down the apartment stairs, disappointed, a little worried.

At home, she found her mother, just returned from Brunswick. "Did you have a good time?" Sandy asked.

"It always does me good to visit your aunt Mary. What about you?"

"The game and company went well." She paused. "But Jeff didn't really seem himself all weekend."

"What do you mean?"

She didn't say that he hadn't wanted to make love with her that evening. "At the game, he was just preoccupied, not very sociable. He went off for over an hour and left us—and with his mother and uncle and his uncle's friend there."

"That is strange."

"He said he was okay, but I think maybe he wasn't feeling well."

Sandy was about to suggest they have a cup of hot tea and go to bed when she heard a car pull up and steps on the front porch. She stood up and looked out of the window. "Oh—it's Bill."

He was about to ring the bell when Sandy opened the door. "Another surprise visit?"

"Actually I—I saw your two cars parked in the driveway and thought I'd stop. I wanted to talk to you both."

"Come in, sit down," said Mrs. Harris. "Can I get you something to drink?"

"No, thanks." They all sat in the living room, and the women looked questioningly at him. "I'm sorry to burst in on you like this," he said, "but there's something you should know."

"What is it?" Mrs. Harris asked.

"I was at the game with Frank Golden yesterday— my Atlanta friend from UNC. We saw Jeff there. I don't know where you were, Sandy."

"Jeff and I weren't together the whole time."

"Well, I don't know how to say this." Bill shifted his feet nervously. "Frank sometimes—so many kids do it—he sometimes smokes pot. He knows where to get it in Atlanta. While we were walking around before the game, we noticed Jeff standing behind one of those portable bathrooms they'd set up. Frank said, 'Oh, my God, there's my old drug dealer.' Then we saw this strange-looking guy go back there to him. Frank said, 'I know that guy too. That's a supplier named Elgin.' This Elgin character and Jeff talked a couple minutes and then, fast as a snake, Elgin just disappeared back into the crowd."

Sandy could feel the blood draining from her face.

"What are you saying, Bill?" asked Mrs. Harris.

"I think Jeff is dealing here at Georgia."

Sandy's eyes sparked. "I know why you're telling us both this. You've wanted us to think badly of Jeff ever since he came back to Athens."

Bill turned to her. "I know you don't like that news, but you shouldn't blame the messenger. I'm telling you for your own good. I care about you." He looked at her mother. "I care about you both."

Mrs. Harris began to speak, but Sandy cut her off. "Thank you for your concern. And now that you've delivered your message, you'd better leave."

Bill stood and walked to the door, Sandy following him. "I understand this is a shock," he said. "We can talk more about this later, when you've had time…"

"There will be no need for that," said Sandy.

"Goodbye, Bill." She opened the door. He went out and down the porch steps.

"Wait, Bill," cried her mother. She jumped up and ran after him. Sandy watched as she caught up to Bill and embraced him, then close to his ear, seemed to speak reassuringly to him.

Sandy turned away from the door, afraid she might have to go to the guest room and be sick again. So Elgin was not in jail after all.

Chapter Thirteen

In the bathroom, her heart pounding, Sandy took deep breaths. She understood now why Jeff had not been himself during the weekend. The police must have wanted him to continue to meet with Elgin, to get more information on him. And they'd had a meeting at the game—while all his family was there.

Sandy left the bathroom as her mother came back into the house. "Bill was right," Mrs. Harris said. "You didn't need to blame the messenger. He was just trying to help." She put her arm around Sandy. "I understand why you're upset, honey. I'd come to care about Jeff, too. It's a shock to us both, even though I'd been afraid...I'm so, so sorry. I suppose Bill and his friend will go to the police about this."

Sandy pulled away. "I have to call him."

"Why? To warn him?"

Sandy didn't answer. She merely grabbed her purse and rushed upstairs, where she pulled out her phone, and tapped on Jeff's name.

He picked up right away. "Hey," he greeted her. His voice sounded better now, strong. "I was just going to call you. I've been thinking. We only have a few days until classes start. I'd like to go for a hike on the Appalachian Trail tomorrow."

Sandy did not expect that. "You would?"

"I'll pick you up at eight. Don't worry about food. We'll pick up something at the deli for a picnic. Oh— and Sandy—be sure to bring your Nikon—and your telescopic lens."

The camera with the big lens would be heavy for hiking. "You really want to do this?"

"I do. I'm sorry about the way I acted this weekend. I'll explain tomorrow."

"Wait, Jeff." She gripped the phone tighter and lowered her voice. "You won't need to explain. I know they haven't arrested Elgin. I know you met with him at the game."

He was silent for a moment. Then he said, "How did you find out?"

"Bill came by just now. He said he and his friend Frank saw you with Elgin at the game. Frank recognized him as a supplier and you as his old drug contact."

"*Frank* recognized Elgin, huh?" Jeff asked wryly. "Yes, I met him at the game. I was wearing a wire again. It was a brief meeting—I can't believe anyone saw us." He stopped for a moment. "Well, maybe it's good you know he's still on the loose. I didn't tell you because I didn't want you to worry."

"Now I know why you disappeared."

"I've done some research tonight. I have a plan that will get this over with and put Elgin in jail. I'll tell you on the hike tomorrow."

****

It had been like old times for the past hour, walking behind Jeff on the trail, the dappled sunshine on their shoulders, the earth firm as they stepped over the stones and roots under their feet. They'd had their picnic before they started, and now Jeff seemed confident as he strode before her. The peaceful, natural setting around her was a contrast to the frightening story Jeff had told her—that Elgin wanted Jeff to start dealing meth. He had a manufacturing lab out in the country. He hadn't given the specific location of the site, but Jeff thought he had figured it out from the few facts Elgin had dropped at the game. He wanted to scout out that area on their hike—test his theory.

"It will be safe," he said. "We'll stay at a distance. But if I can spot their lab, I can alert Terrisi and maybe get this finished sooner. I want you to take some photos with your telescopic lens. Would you be willing to do that? If you don't want to, we'll just go back home."

"I'll do anything to help," Sandy had replied.

And so here they were, on the trail which Jeff was sure would eventually overlook the farm valley where Elgin's lab was located.

"Here," Jeff said, suddenly stopping. He pulled a sketched map from his pocket, studied it briefly, and turned to the woods.

She knew they were supposed to stay on the trail. "We're going into the woods here?"

"Just come with me." Jeff brushed aside branches and pushed into the woods. She followed. After a few minutes of struggling through thick understory growth, they came out onto the edge of the mountain. Jeff looked down into the valley below. "I was right. I'm sure this is it. Get your camera ready."

She checked the settings. He stood beside her, put his arm over her shoulders, and pointed. "See that farmhouse and the barns down there?"

Sandy looked at the decrepit house with its sagging

front porch and the ramshackle barns behind it, like toys in the distance. "Yes."

"See if you can get some closeup shots of them."

Sandy raised the camera and focused. The house came up close and clear. It was badly in need of paint and unremarkable, not architecturally interesting. She took some pictures, then moved her viewer to the barns and took some shots of them.

"Can you take some videos?"

"Yes, but nothing's going on down there."

"Keep watching."

Seeing a car drive up a rutted dirt road to the house, she raised her camera and began videoing. The car stopped, the door opened, and a tall, thin man in black got out. "Who is that?" she asked, the camera still running.

"It's Elgin."

Her heart skipped a beat.

"They manufacture meth in that farmhouse. Your videos will be enough to show the detectives where to find the lab. And they'll recognize Elgin."

The front door to the farmhouse opened and another tall, thin figure stepped out. "Oh, my God," Sandy said. She turned the lens, pulling the view of that figure in even closer. "It's—Bill."

"Keep videoing."

The two men spoke on the porch for a moment, then walked into the house. Sandy paused the video and turned, shocked, to Jeff. "What is Bill doing there?"

"What do you think?"

"But he goes to the University of North Carolina. He hasn't been home for four years except on short vacations. How can he be involved with drugs here?"

"They sell drugs at UNC, too. Bill must be one of Elgin's dealers up there. He must have met Elgin through Frank."

As Sandy turned back to the view below, she saw the two men re-emerge onto the farmhouse porch. They seemed to be scrutinizing the landscape. Did one of them have binoculars? Then they turned to the mountain—yes, Elgin was pointing binoculars toward them. Jeff said abruptly, "Shit, let's go." He turned and led the way back, fast, to the trail.

Sandy, breathless, hustled to keep up. "Do you think they saw us?"

"I don't know. We'd better just go to the car and get back to Athens. We need to download your pictures and send them to Terrisi."

In spite of their fast-walking pace, it was about an hour before they arrived at the trailhead next to the parking lot. Jeff held out an arm and stopped Sandy from leaving the safety of the trees. "Let's check and see who's out there." He scanned the parked cars, then turned to Sandy. "Better give me your camera."

She handed it to him. He shrugged off his outer shirt and wrapped the camera in it. Seeing a large hollow log nearby, he stuck it inside. Then he put some leafy branches over the open end of the log. "I'll get the car and bring it over here to the trailhead. If it's all clear, you get the camera and come on."

"Jeff, you're scaring me."

"Don't be scared, honey. I'm just trying to be safe." He gave her a quick kiss, then stepped out onto the edge of the parking lot. He looked around, then jogged to his car. Sandy watched. When Jeff reached his SUV, she saw someone rise up from behind it—the thin man in black. Elgin.

Heart pounding, she ducked back into the leaves, only to have sinewy arms grab her from behind. A hand clamped over her mouth, and a familiar-sounding voice spoke. "It's okay. Just stay quiet." The tight hold prevented any struggle. In a minute, a car pulled up to the entrance of the trailhead. The person who had grabbed her pushed her out of the woods. He reached around her, opened the back door, shoved her in, and got in beside her. Yes, as she'd guessed: it was Bill. He must have been hiding there in the woods right where she and Jeff would come out.

Elgin sat behind the wheel, Jeff in the passenger seat. Elgin drove off. "Good work, Morrison," he said. "So, Hudson, I guess you wanted to see where we make the meth. I wasn't expecting you. Bill here was at least invited and on schedule."

"Sandy and I were hiking. I thought I knew where you were talking about at the game, and I just wanted to take a look from the trail." He indicated Sandy. "She doesn't know anything."

"Well, I'll show you both the lab now, okay? Morrison, I believe you and Hudson already know each other. You and he met up with me at the same time in Atlanta during Christmas vacation a couple years ago, remember?"

Bill kept his eyes averted from Sandy. "You're right. But Jeff and I already knew each other. We went to the same grade school."

"*You* told Elgin I was at the University of Georgia, didn't you?" Jeff said. "Damn you, Morrison!"

Bill did not reply. He leaned toward Elgin in the front seat. "So we're going back to the farm now?"

Elgin laughed. "We sure are." He drove down the side of the mountain and onto a small country dirt road, which he followed until they came to the buildings Sandy had photographed. Elgin got out and opened the passenger side door for Jeff. It was then Sandy saw he was holding a gun. "Come in, be our guests."

"Have a seat," he told them as they entered the house. There was a strange smell inside, and a few bare chairs in what once must have been a living room. Elgin waved his gun, and Sandy and Jeff each sat in a chair, dropping their backpacks on the floor nearby.

Elgin turned to Sandy. "You took pictures with a fancy camera up there? Where is it?"

Jeff spoke up. "She doesn't have the camera."

The man moved toward Sandy. "Where is it?"

Sandy's mind was whirling, trying to think of an answer. But all she could say was, "I don't know."

Jeff quickly spoke again. "I was carrying it. We were rushing to get back to the trailhead. The neck strap broke along the way. I didn't realize right away. It must be somewhere along the trail."

Elgin drew back his hand and slapped Jeff hard across the face. "You better come up with a more believable story than that." He turned to Bill. "Did you see what they did with the camera?"

Bill shook his head. "The trees blocked my view."

Elgin checked his phone, walked to the door, and looked out. He turned to Bill. "I have to meet a contact at the end of the road." He handed him the gun. "You know how to shoot this?"

"Sure."

"You watch these two. I'll be back in a couple of minutes, and we'll figure out what to do with them."

"Yes, sir," said Bill. His freckles stood out against his abnormally pale face. Elgin left.

Sandy panicked. She thought of people going missing on the Appalachian Trail, of the drug-ring-related murders she'd read about. She looked to Bill. "What's he going to do with us?"

"I don't know," Bill answered. Then, "I've never been here before either. I swear. I was just supposed to meet him here and get some meth to bring back to North Carolina."

"Using that business degree, huh?" said Jeff. "Going to sell and make a little money?"

"Like you," said Bill.

"What do you get? Fifty for each tab of Adderall or a cartridge? Same for a few grams of grass? Then split with Elgin?"

"Something like that."

"And now the meth too, huh?"

Sandy spoke up. "Ironic that you warned me about Jeff all those times, isn't it? Saying how much better you'd be for me. And you told me it was *Frank* at the game who recognized Elgin and what was happening."

Bill looked at Sandy now. "I know." His voice was low. "I've hidden a lot—from you, from my parents, even from Frank. Frank introduced me to Elgin just by chance one time, and he and I have done dope together, but he never knew I saw Elgin again and started dealing...I do have limits, Sandy. I didn't do anything but grass and carts, and amphetamines only at exam time. I didn't want anything to do with this meth Elgin's gotten into. That's stuff's poison. But Elgin was going to make me bring some to a North Carolina dealer when I went back. I was going to be his mule."

"Bill, you aren't like him," Sandy said. "Help get us out of here. He might kill us."

"I bet you wouldn't be the first." Bill hesitated for a moment, then walked to the door and looked down the road. Turning back, he said, "There's another road behind the barns. I left my car parked there. Here are the keys." He tossed them to Jeff. "When I'm sure Elgin's far enough away, Hudson—punch me and grab the gun. Then you two go through the kitchen and out the back door. Take my car and follow that road. It takes you to the state highway."

"Thank you!" Sandy breathed.

"Thanks, man," said Jeff.

Bill glanced at him. "I'm not doing this for you." He walked to the door, looked out, then turned back to them. "Okay, he's gone."

Jeff rose from the chair, raised his fist, and gave Bill's jaw a resounding crack. Bill was thrown back against the wall. He put his hand to his jaw, shook his head as if to clear it, then focused his pale, green eyes on Jeff and Sandy. "Go!"

They picked up their backpacks, Jeff grabbed the gun from Bill, and they ran through the kitchen, with its big, now empty, caldrons on the stove, and out the back door. Behind the barns, Sandy saw the familiar red sports car. "This is it," she said. They jumped in, Jeff punched the ignition button, and they sped down the road as Bill had directed.

When they reached the paved highway, Sandy began to breathe more easily. "I hope Elgin won't suspect Bill *let* us escape."

"That's why I punched him so hard," Jeff said. "It had to look real."

"What do we do now?"

"Call Terrisi." He gestured toward his backpack on the floor at her feet. "His number's on my phone. He and his partner can go up to the trailhead and get the camera out of that log. They'll find enough evidence on it and in the farmhouse to get that bastard Elgin and his partner put away for a long time."

"What will they do to Bill?"

"I think when we explain how he helped us escape and if he testifies against Elgin, he'll get off with a pretty light sentence."

****

Fall semester classes were to begin the following week, on a Wednesday. That Tuesday evening, Jeff and Sandy joined their friends, who knew nothing of what had passed, in the large circular booth at Ruggeri's. "To our last free evening," said Will, holding up his mug.

"To the last free evening!" chorused the others.

"Look, here comes Bill," said Tom. "Hey, Bill!"

Sandy looked up as Bill approached. His jaw was still slightly swollen and black and blue. Seeing him, all that had happened in the last week flashed through her mind. Terrisi had retrieved her camera, found the meth lab, and arrested Elgin and his partner. They were now really in jail, and the detectives were pursuing others in the ring. Bill had been questioned and let out on bond. His parents were shocked to learn of what he'd been doing, but he promised them never to take or deal again. He'd also agreed to testify against Elgin. His lawyer thought he might be granted witness immunity—or certainly leniency in light of his role in Sandy and Jeff's escape. Sandy had not told her mother anything about Bill, but once she explained about Jeff working with the police and discovering the location of the lab, Mrs. Harris again regarded Jeff as a hero. Jeff's father and Uncle Jake decided it would be best not to tell his mother the story, but they, too, were proud of him, impressed with what he had done.

As Bill stopped at the booth, the group noticed a short, young man with red hair and muscular shoulders, sort of like Jeff's, at his side.

"Hey!" Bill said. "You-all, this is Frank Golden. He's a friend from the University of North Carolina. He lives in Atlanta, and we're going to drive back to Chapel Hill together."

Frank grinned and saluted them.

"Join us—we can squeeze in two more," said Kathy.

"No, thanks. Frank and I have to talk about our travel plans." Bill and his friend went to a smaller booth and sat down, bending their heads toward each other across the table.

Members of a little band began tuning up at the back of the store, and soon they began their first piece. As fast music pulsated about them, Sandy saw Bill leave Frank and come to their big booth. He looked rather shyly at Jeff. "Do you mind if I ask Sandy to dance?"

"No, go ahead," Jeff replied. "You're the better dancer."

Sandy felt relieved. Maybe she and Bill could be friends again. Maybe even Jeff and Bill would be friends someday. She slid out of the booth. Dancing with Bill brought back old, more innocent times. When the band stopped playing, he stood facing her. She wondered what to say, but he spoke first, almost casually. "So you and Kathy have moved into your new apartment?"

"Yes. My mother didn't mind. She's doing much better now, I think. She'll go back to work next week." She paused, trying to be equally casual. "Can you come by tomorrow and see the apartment?"

"I can't, sorry. Frank and I are leaving early in the morning. We're actually going to take a trip in the Smokies and stay a couple of nights. Then I'll take him on to Chapel Hill."

"That sounds like a nice trip."

Bill lowered his voice. "I'll be back. I have to postpone getting my MBA. My dad says I can keep on working for him in the store. There will be the hearing, legal stuff to straighten out, trials. I don't know what will happen. My parents and I would pay any fine, but I may have to do time for dealing."

"Without you, Elgin might not have been caught. And who knows what would have happened to Jeff and me? Plus, you'll be testifying against Elgin. I'm sure you'll just be put on parole. Maybe you can get your MBA next year—if you want to."

Bill nodded. He still looked serious. "But it's time to tell you something else."

Sandy felt a wave of apprehension. "What?"

"I lived with Frank the summer I was in Spain. We were…a couple. I came home thinking this summer I would try to be what my parents wanted me to be. I'd quit doing pot and cards, work in the store, date you." He looked at her intently. "But dating you wasn't just for my parents. It was for myself, too. I figured if I could get involved with any girl, it would be you. But I learned you can't change who you are. Maybe that's why I started doing drugs in the first place. I was stressed, trying to figure myself out. When Elgin contacted me, I sold to make myself more financially independent from my parents in case..." His voice trailed off.

Sandy felt shock waves run through her at this revelation. Everything about Bill fell into place. Why he'd always seemed like only a brother to her. Why in grade school he had wanted so much to fight in that physical, love-hate boyhood ritual. Why that attempt to kiss her this summer had felt like an experiment.

Bill regarded her with warmth in his eyes. "You will always be my best *girl*, Sandy."

She was surprised at how quickly the world snapped back into place. She reached out and touched his hand. "Much as our parents wanted it, you and I were not meant to be."

His worried look came back. "I haven't told my mother and father about Frank and me yet. They've had enough to cope with. I don't know when I will or how they'll react."

"I'm sure they'll understand. They love you."

"There's all the kids here, too, and your mom...Even if they never know about my dealing, they'll have to know about this."

Sandy thought about her mother's image of Bill as the perfect son-in-law for her. She remembered the *Pride and Prejudice* theme of how different actual reality often is from what one imagines. But she could not express all that now or ever.

All she could say was, "They care about you too. The kind of relationship you and Frank have is becoming accepted now. I think everything will be fine." She paused. "He must be a nice guy."

"He is," replied Bill. "And I guess Jeff is also." He gave her a quick kiss on the cheek. "I promise I'll stay in better touch."

Jeff came over and joined them. "Bill's leaving tomorrow for a trip to the mountains and then Chapel Hill," Sandy told him. "He'll be back for the hearing."

Jeff extended his hand. "Good luck. I'll do what I can to help."

Bill took it. "Thanks." The two young men regarded each other with what seemed, Sandy thought, a kind of mutual respect at last. Then Bill said, "I've kept Frank waiting long enough. I'll see both of you soon." He headed back to the booth where his friend waited.

They watched him go. Then Sandy turned to Jeff and said simply, "It's Bill and Frank."

Jeff looked over at the two talking, their heads bent close, their hands touching on the tabletop. "I see."

He put his arm around her and pulled her close.

Epilogue

Two Years Later

"You look lovely." Mrs. Harris regarded the wreath of white flowers on Sandy's hair, smoothed the long, satin skirt of her wedding gown, and adjusted the lace veil one more time. As she stepped back to admire her daughter, they became aware of the organ music sounding from the church sanctuary.

A light knock sounded on the dressing room door, and Uncle Tim said, "It's time."

"Are you nervous, sweetheart?"

"No, not really, Mom. This just seems right."

"That's because it is right. You'll be very happy together."

Sandy nodded. She and Jeff had earned their degrees. While he and his uncle grew the fruits and vegetables on Rushing Creek Farm, she would be working as a freelance photojournalist, traveling to news events in their area of the state with the farm as her base. She'd also use her skills to publicize Rushing Creek far more than Uncle Jake had. Sibyl would be visiting often, for Ash had offered to pick her up and fly her to North Carolina whenever he came to Atlanta on business. And of course, Jeff and Sandy would go regularly to see Dr. Hudson, Glenda, Bobby, and

Sandy's mother in Athens, the place where everything had begun.

Mrs. Harris handed Sandy the bouquet of summer flowers from the nearby table and opened the door to speak to her brother-in-law. "She's ready. So am I."

"Then it's time to take your seat," he said.

Bill, in his groomsman tuxedo, stood waiting there as well. He crooked his arm to escort Mrs. Harris down the aisle, past the crowded pews to the front, where on the right Sandy's aunt Mary was already sitting. In the row behind them were Bill's parents and Frank. Across the aisle sat Jeff's mother with his grandparents and Ash. In the pew behind them were Dr. Hudson, Glenda, and an excited five-year-old Bobby. After seating Sandy's mother, Bill joined Will Thompson, Uncle Jake, and Jeff, who were standing at the front of the sanctuary. Uncle Jake would serve as Jeff's best man.

Sandy's uncle Tim watched and when everyone was in place, nodded at her. She stepped through the door and took his arm. Ahead of her in long, yellow dresses and also holding bouquets of summer flowers stood her maid of honor, Kathy, and her bridesmaids, Carole Connolly and Diane Miller. The preliminary organ music paused, then struck up the dramatic initial notes of Mendelssohn's *Wedding March.*

Diane, the first in line, began the slow, measured walk down the aisle, followed by Carol, then Kathy, and finally, Sandy and Uncle Tim. As they approached the front of the sanctuary, her eyes met Jeff's, golden and glowing as she had seen them so often.

He was smiling at her. She smiled back.

A word about the author...

Patricia McAlexander earned a bachelor's degree from The University of New York at Albany, a master's from Columbia University, and a doctorate from The University of Wisconsin, Madison, all in English. After moving with her husband to Athens, Georgia, she taught composition and literature at The University of Georgia. Now retired, she has edited local newsletters and enjoys hiking, travel, and photography. But most of all she enjoys writing novels. Her thriller-romance *Stranger in the Storm* was released by Wild Rose in June 2020.

Author's Note

I hope you enjoyed *Shadows of Doubt*—and if you haven't yet read my first novel, *Stranger in the Storm,* you might enjoy it also.

People often ask where I get ideas for my stories. For an answer, I think of those kaleidoscopes from my childhood, with glass-like fragments that change position when you turn the lens. You look through the scope and watch the shifting fragments form new designs. The fragments are like my memories and observations, transformed into new patterns for my stories. The settings are an example. My first novel, *Stranger in the Storm*, takes place mostly on the Great Sacandaga Lake in the Adirondacks of upstate New York, where my parents had a summer cottage and dairy farms dotted the countryside nearby. The main character, Janet Mitchell, goes there to escape an abusive relationship and meets the mysterious young man who rescues her during the storm of the title. As I wrote the novel, visions of its setting came to me as sharply as the original upon which they were based.

Shadows of Doubt takes place in the town where I live now—Athens, Georgia. Here in close juxtaposition are the University of Georgia campus with its carnival-like football-game Saturdays in the fall, quiet family neighborhoods, a forest park lake, and mountain hiking trails not far away. All of these scenes, with of course some modification, are found in the novel.

For advice on early drafts of *Shadows of Doubt*, I thank my sister, Dorothy Altman, herself a fine creative writer; my good friend Jane Marston, an amazing poet; and my husband Hubert, retired Professor of American

Literature at the University of Georgia. My Wild Rose editor Kaycee John, with her keen eye for plot and style, also made excellent suggestions. Finally, my great-nephew Isaac Altman gave me his insights as a high school student into the youth drug culture that is so important in this novel.

I love to hear from my readers. You can contact me at mcalexanderpatricia@gmail.com. To find out more about me and what I'm working on, check out my website at https://patriciamcalexander.weebly.com or my Facebook Author Page, Patricia McAlexander, Author. And please consider leaving a review of my novels on Amazon and Goodreads.

Thank you for purchasing
this publication of The Wild Rose Press, Inc.

For questions or more information
contact us at
info@thewildrosepress.com.

The Wild Rose Press, Inc.
www.thewildrosepress.com